Lady Abigail's Perfect Match

The Townsbridges, Volume 2

Sophie Barnes

Published by Sophie Barnes, 2019.

LADY ABIGAIL'S PERFECT MATCH

The Townsbridges

Copyright © 2019 by Sophie Barnes

All Rights Reserved. No part of this book may be used or reproduced by any means, graphic, electronic, or mechanical, including photocopying, recording, taping, or by any information storage retrieval system without the written permission of the publisher except in the case of brief quotations embodied in critical articles and reviews.

This is a work of fiction. Names, characters, places and incidents are either the product of the author's imagination or used in a fictitious manner. Any resemblance to actual persons, living or dead, business establishments, actual events or locales is purely coincidental.

Cover design by The Killion Group

By Sophie Barnes

Novels

The Forgotten Duke
More Than A Rogue
The Infamous Duchess
No Ordinary Duke
The Illegitimate Duke
The Girl Who Stepped Into The Past
The Duke of Her Desire
Christmas at Thorncliff Manor
A Most Unlikely Duke
His Scandalous Kiss
The Earl's Complete Surrender
Lady Sarah's Sinful Desires
The Danger in Tempting an Earl
The Scandal in Kissing an Heir
The Trouble with Being a Duke
The Secret Life of Lady Lucinda
There's Something About Lady Mary
Lady Alexandra's Excellent Adventure
How Miss Rutherford Got Her Groove Back

Novellas

When Love Leads To Scandal
Miss Compton's Christmas Romance
The Duke Who Came To Town
The Earl Who Loved Her
The Governess Who Captured His Heart
Mistletoe Magic (from Five Golden Rings: A Christmas Collection)

Chapter One

MARRIAGE.

For most of the young men with whom James Townsbridge was acquainted, this was the most dreaded word in the English language. For James himself, however, the word was synonymous with comfort and joy, loyalty and love. After all, his parents were happily married and so was his older brother, Charles. He and Bethany, his wife of two years, made no secret about the fact they adored each other. So James always found it strange when his friends spoke of eventually 'doing their duty' with dread in their eyes and as if they were waiting for some terrifying fate to befall them.

Granted, James could appreciate the fact that marriages of convenience existed, that they could result in mismatched husbands and wives, and that he would be able to avoid such a dreadful catastrophe with greater ease than some of the other bachelors London had to offer. After all, he wasn't the heir to anything, and as such, he could be more liberal when choosing his bride.

The most important thing, in his estimation, was to pick wisely. And since he was now six and twenty, the same age Charles had been when he married Bethany, James had decided it was time to start looking for the right woman with whom to spend the rest of his life.

With this in mind, he maintained a constant awareness of all the young ladies arriving in the Pratchard ballroom while trying to ignore the crippling headache he'd had all day. As a result, his attention to the conversation going on around him was limited, making his sister Athena's comment about a diamond-encrusted wig and butterfly wings sound completely nonsensical.

"It's a bit predictable, isn't it?" inquired James's younger brother, William.

"What about a dress entwined by ivy?" James's other sister, Sarah, suggested. "You'd look like an ancient ruin, which I believe would be far more original."

Athena clapped her hands together. "Oh yes." She beamed as though she'd just discovered Atlantis, and for a moment, James managed to ignore the fact that his brain felt as though it were being run over by a carriage.

Honestly, he ought to have stayed home in bed. Better yet, he should have refrained from getting foxed last night. But he'd been out, celebrating the final moments of Mr. Hugh Ravenough's freedom. And as Hugh's longtime friend, he didn't want to miss the celebration.

"With a bird perched on my head."

James blinked. "What?" He stared at Athena in stupefied wonder. Clearly, he had missed something, or perhaps she'd finally taken that extra step required to enter pure insanity. Or maybe his blasted headache made it impossible for him to understand basic conversation.

He eyed William to gauge his reaction and saw that he was grinning. And then he said, "I could bring shears."

James sighed while Sarah, Athena, and William laughed like a mob of mad pixies.

Oh, if only he'd been paying attention. And if only his head didn't ache as if it were being beaten by spiky clubs wielded by an army of angry trolls.

"I don't believe I've met her before," Sarah was now saying in a lower voice.

"Who?" James forced himself to ask so he could follow this new subject of conversation. But rather than answer, Sarah glanced toward the left. James shifted his gaze and instinctively straightened his back. Approaching were the Marquess and Marchioness of Foxborough. They appeared to be accompanying a young lady whom he'd never seen before.

James considered her as he had so many others. She wasn't exactly beautiful – at least not in the classical sense – but she wasn't plain either. Her hair was neither blonde nor brown, and while he initially found her face to be too round, he decided it suited her and that he rather liked her features. In fact, upon further consideration, he had to acknowledge that he would be hard pressed to find a better mouth than hers. It was just right: softly curved at the top and full on the bottom.

What James did not like, however, was the hint of displeasure in the young lady's eyes and the stiffness with which she carried herself. Everything about her seemed to say, "I'd rather be anywhere else but here."

"Good evening," Lord Foxborough said. James and his siblings greeted the marquess and marchioness politely then prepared themselves for the inevitable introduction. "I would like to present our daughter, Lady Abigail." His expression was warm and inviting – the exact opposite of Lady Abigail's. Indeed, her frozen features made her look more like a painting than a real flesh and blood person. It also gave her a certain aloofness that James didn't care for.

"A pleasure," Athena said. "I am Miss Athena and this is my older sister, Miss Townsbridge."

"Delighted," Sarah added.

William bowed and murmured a very distinct, "Enchanted," to which James almost rolled his eyes.

And then it was his turn to speak. Only the moment happened to coincide with another sharp stab to his skull. He gritted his teeth and felt his entire face tighten up in response to the pain. "Ugh," he grunted, earning a stunned look of surprise from everyone except Lady Abigail, who was now studying the floor. Wincing, he gave a stiff nod in acknowledgement of the introduction while biting back another guttural response to the horrid sensation of having nails driven into his head. If it hadn't been for his mother insisting he make an appearance, he'd be home in bed.

"Our daughter isn't acquainted with many young ladies her own age," Lady Foxborough said. She scowled at James before returning her attention to his sisters. "We tend to favor the country, you see, but since the time has come for her to make her debut, we have no choice but to spend more time here in Town." She smiled and a brief moment of awkward silence followed.

Until Sarah said, "Perhaps we can take a turn about the room together, Lady Abigail?"

Lady Abigail gave an almost indistinct nod. "Yes," she whispered in a strained voice that made her lack of enthusiasm clear.

James's dislike of her doubled. She might be a marquess's daughter, but he and his sisters were Viscount George Roxley's children. And while it was true that Charles had caused a bit of a scandal two years ago when he'd stolen his friend's fiancée, and Society was only now starting to forget Athena's involvement in this, Lady Abigail ought to be pleased with the prospect of keeping their company. She should at the very least have thanked Sarah for the offer.

But since she hadn't, James decided right then and there that he would rather be elsewhere. Somewhere far away from Lady Abigail's upturned nose. Especially since he was barely able to think on account of his headache. Lord, he really should have stayed home tonight.

The very thought of a blissfully silent room shrouded in darkness was almost enough to make him sigh with longing. "Excuse me," he heard himself say in a tone that sounded far more annoyed than he had intended. And then, taking a step back, he glanced at his siblings and said, "I have to go." Upon which he simply left, leaving them to apologize on his behalf.

A little surprised by the lack of guilt he felt over being so rude, James quit the ballroom and sought out the nearest sanctuary. Perhaps a brief rest would help ease his suffering. Perhaps, if he felt better later, he'd ask Lady Abigail to dance to make up for his lack of good manners.

Or perhaps he'd simply forget having met her.

Now there was something worth hoping for, he decided as he sneaked inside a dark room and closed the door behind him.

WHAT A HORRID MAN.

Abigail still couldn't fathom how poorly Mr. James Townsbridge had treated not only herself but her parents. By contrast, his sisters were a delight. Even Mr. William Townsbridge, who seemed to be quite a bit younger, had proven far more courteous than his older brother. He'd even signed her dance card, for which she was very grateful, since she'd always enjoyed dancing.

But Mr. James Townsbridge...

She'd seen him for the first time three years ago when she and her parents had spent a brief time in London while Parliament was in session. Her father usually came to Town by himself whenever business required it, but that time, he'd brought his family with him. And during one warm spring day while riding by carriage through Hyde Park, Abigail had spotted him - the most handsome man she'd ever seen in her life.

He'd been walking with his sisters she realized now after having met Miss Townsbridge and Lady Athena. And he'd been smiling in response to something they were saying, which had instantly caused a bubbly sensation in the pit of Abigail's belly. At fifteen she'd been smitten, and had looked for Mr. Townsbridge again when she'd come to Town last Christmas.

This time, she'd encountered him at the theatre where he'd been seated in a box almost directly opposite her, together with his entire family. Since then, she'd daydreamed about her coming out and him gallantly inviting her to dance. But of course this was just a dream, because when it actually came to meeting the man, her stomach had starting flopping around until she'd feared she might be sick all over him or one of his siblings. And her heart had been pounding too, while a wave of uncomfortable heat crept over her skin. Putting on a smile and pretending she was all right had proven a challenge. Speech had been near impossible.

And her illusion about James Townsbridge himself had shattered.

She'd sensed his dislike of her right from the start. With one singular glance he'd found her lacking. Well, she disliked him as well now, though this acknowledgement didn't make her feel any better. On the contrary it was rather depressing.

"You must excuse our brother's deplorable manners," Miss Townsbridge said as they made their way along the periphery of the room.

"He was being a twit," Miss Athena added with such forceful certainty that Abigail had to press her lips together in order not to laugh. She liked the youngest member of the Townsbridge family very much, even though she would never confess to sharing her opinion of her brother.

"It's a pity you had to experience him like this," Miss Townsbridge remarked. "He's usually agreeable and a great deal of fun to be around. Which probably explains his immense popularity."

At this, Abigail snorted. It happened involuntarily and caught her by surprise. Like a sneeze. "Sorry," she said, except the word did not leave her mouth with even the slightest bit of sincerity. Instead, it was mumbled under her breath while heat rushed into her cheeks.

Miss Townsbridge and Miss Athena looked at her with raised eyebrows. And then Miss Athena said, "Do you have any brothers, Lady Abigail?"

Abigail nodded. "Lance is three years older than I," she said, hoping to leave it at that. But of course the information she'd supplied wasn't enough for her two new friends. They wanted details. And as Abigail provided the answers to a seemingly endless list of questions, her annoyance with their brother faded and she began to relax.

"So he's not without flaws, then, is he?" Miss Townsbridge politely inquired when they'd all finished laughing over Abigail's account about Lance's once swinging a door open so hard it hit their younger sister, Petra, smack in the face.

"Of course not," Abigail said.

Miss Athena smiled. "Perhaps you will keep that in mind before you judge our own brother too harshly. Poor judgment doesn't necessarily denote poor character."

And just like that, having been put firmly in her place, the calm sense of ease Abigail had enjoyed for the last few minutes abandoned her completely. Her face burned with shame and her eyes began to prick with the realization that she had ruined the chance she'd had of being friends with these women. They thought her too critical of others, and perhaps they were right.

Perhaps it hadn't been her but something else that had caused him to act as he had.

"I'm sorry," she said while embarrassment snaked its way around her, squeezing her until she knew she had to escape. So she took a step back, and then another. "Please forgive me. I meant no offense."

"Oh indeed, we did not mean to imply..." Miss Townsbridge began. A look of concern marred her features.

But now that Abigail was already fleeing, it seemed there was no stopping her retreat. Without waiting to hear the rest of Miss Townsbridge's sentence, she spun around and quickened her pace. The nervousness Mr. James Townsbridge had evoked returned, and the supper she'd had at home earlier in the evening began climbing up her throat. It was much too hot and overcrowded; the thick smell of perfume mixed with candle wax and roses put on display, making the air hard to breathe.

Desperately, Abigail glanced toward the doors leading out to the terrace. Fresh air and privacy existed beyond them. But only if she managed to circumvent the crowd blocking her path.

Her skin pricked in response to the sheen of moisture that started to gather between her shoulder blades. She sucked in a breath and felt her throat constrict in response to the stuffy heat.

Guided by her reflexes, she hurried through an archway leading out to the hallway beyond the ballroom. The air was better out here but the need to find solace in a place where she could gather her thoughts and her composure without being disturbed made her head toward a closed door a little farther along.

She tried the handle and the door gave way, opening toward a room where black shadows hid the walls. Only a purple hue entering through a tall window offered some semblance of light. Fearing the sanctuary she had just found would be snatched from her grasp if she lingered in the doorway, Abigail slipped quickly inside and closed the door.

A wave of relief washed over her, cooling her and offering comfort. Her muscles relaxed, teasing away the nausea she'd felt since coming face to face with Mr. James Townsbridge. The silence that filled the room was blessed indeed, and she savored it as she crossed to the window and opened the latch to a welcome waft of cool air. She inhaled deeply through her nose and was instantly rewarded with the fresh smell of jasmine from the garden beyond.

With a sigh, she smoothed the white muslin skirt of her gown and turned her gaze on the room behind her. The furniture stood silhouetted like irregular shapes emerging from the darkness. Identifying what appeared to be a sofa, Abigail made her way toward it, muttering lightly beneath her breath when her shin connected with a corner table. She went around it, moving her feet with small careful steps in case there were other obstacles in her path.

Locating the sofa's armrest, she walked her fingers along its length until she was certain she had a solid hold. She then turned and sat, momentarily caught off guard by the uneven lumpiness beneath her. Until the lumpiness moved and a low voice muttered a curse.

Before she could leap to her feet, something grabbed her and pulled her close, like an octopus dragging its prey down into the depths of the ocean.

Startled, Abigail acted on instinct and screamed.

Chapter Two

IF THERE WAS SOMETHING James had always hated, it was being forced awake before he was ready. But sleeping through the jolt that passed through him the moment a large irregular form landed in his lap was impossible.

Torn from the blissful dream he'd been having of picking up shells along the shore and discovering what appeared to be a treasure chest, he was momentarily disorientated and reached out frantically with both hands. The body in his lap screamed, jarring his headache back to life and causing him to curse with the fury of a man who'd just been stabbed.

The door to the parlor opened, illuminating the room with light from the hallway. James felt an odd tug on his arm but ignored it. Instead, he tried to sit up – just enough to look over the back of the sofa.

"Well," was his father's only remark as he stared at him with wide-eyed dismay. Beside him stood the Marquess of Foxborough with a thunderous expression that caused James to re-examine his current situation.

With a shake of his head meant to clear the cobwebs, he returned his attention to the weight still pressing down onto his lap and realized three things.

One: the object that had awoken him from his slumber was in fact a woman.

Two: the woman was none other than the odious, nose in the air, Lady Abigail.

Three: one of the buttons on his jacket sleeve was caught in a piece of lace attached to her bodice.

Which made him very aware that

Four: she looked like she'd been compromised by him, which

Five: would likely involve an offer of marriage.

James groaned and gave his sleeve a yank, but that only made matters worse. A loud ripping sound followed, accompanied by Lady Abigail's horrified cry as part of the bodice was yanked away to reveal the chemise she wore beneath.

Frantically she scrambled off him – finally – while clutching the flapping piece of lace-covered muslin against her breast. "You....you...you imbecile," she said, sounding just as overbearing and insufferable as James already knew her to be. "This is all *your* fault!"

With a sigh, James stood and rubbed the back of his head where a dull ache hummed down his neck before fanning out over his shoulders. If it wasn't for her torn bodice, he rather imagined Lady Abigail would point a haughty finger at him to accentuate her accusation. Instead, she used both hands to cover herself. James turned to his father whose eyes had sharpened in the way they tended to do when he was trying to find a way out of a conundrum.

As much as James loved him for it, he knew there was no way out of this one except by taking the honorable path.

Not with Foxborough staring at him as if he were a vile little toad tainting his daughter's surroundings. There was no point in explaining what had happened. No reason for excuses now that additional people had gathered behind his father and the marquess.

Accepting his fate, James took a deep breath and said, "I have made Lady Abigail an offer of marriage, and she has honored me with her acceptance."

The lady in question squeaked, but said nothing further, for which James was grateful. Foxborough frowned and stepped farther into the room. James's father followed and the two men soon managed to close the door, effectively shutting out the collection of nosy onlookers who'd been steadily gathering in the hallway.

"You have some nerve," Foxborough snapped as soon as they were alone. "She is a marquess's daughter and you're nothing more than a second son. When I introduced her to you, it was not so you could take advantage half an hour later."

"Hold on one moment," Roxley said, his voice taking on the protective tone of a man who was proud of all his children. "James is a good man."

"As illustrated by the fact that he attempted to seduce my daughter as soon as the chance to do so arose."

"That's not at all what happened," Lady Abigail said, her shocked voice conveying the disgust she felt at the thought of her dear papa assuming she'd lower herself so far as to risk being ruined by a man like James. A second son who would never be able to give her the title she clearly deserved. "I came in here to escape the crowd and...and..."

Her father's expression eased. "Have a seat," he told her gently, "and take some deep breaths. It has been a trying evening for you, my pet."

Trying evening?

Good God. James had just lost his freedom to a careless girl, and her father worried *her* evening had been trying? And why on earth did he speak to her now as if she needed coddling? He glanced at her even though he really didn't want to and saw she actually looked quite ill.

"Are you all right?" he asked, partly out of concern and partly because he wasn't a monster.

"Of course not," she managed while gulping down air. "I now have to marry a...a...a..."

Raising an eyebrow, James turned away, his sympathy for his future wife dissolving at the thought of how that sentence would eventually end. He addressed her father. "My apologies, my lord, but I fear there is no way to save Lady Abigail's reputation except through marriage."

"He's right," Roxley said. "Too many people saw and heard too much. If an announcement isn't issued forthwith, she will be labeled a..." He had the decency to clear his throat instead of adding an actual noun to the end of that sentence. "Now, I know you're not pleased by this turn of events, Foxborough, but you and I are well acquainted, and as such I hope you will trust me when I tell you that I have every intention of making sure James can give your daughter the sort of life she deserves."

"Can he give her a title?" Foxborough growled.

"No. Not that," Roxley told him with no hint of being the least bit ruffled by the other man's higher status. "But I can give him Arlington House and the means by which to support himself and his family."

James gaped at his father. Arlington House was a vast estate, built by his great grandfather, and while it wasn't entailed, James had always imagined it would eventually go to his older brother Charles. "Papa," James said, intent on protesting his father's generosity.

Roxley served him a quelling look and raised his hand. "The matter is settled," he said in that serious tone of his that warned it was futile to argue.

"But—" Lady Abigail said, while James cast her a weary look of exasperation. For one blessed moment, he'd forgotten she was there. She stepped forward now, her face pinched and her palm pressed over her stomach.

James fought the urge to roll his eyes. If she felt queasy at the thought of marrying him, she shouldn't have placed herself on top of him in a dark room and then proceeded to scream.

"Lord Roxley is right, my dear," Foxborough said with a compassionate lilt to his voice. "The matter is settled."

Without saying anything more, Lady Abigail's father shook hands with James's, officially sealing their children's fate.

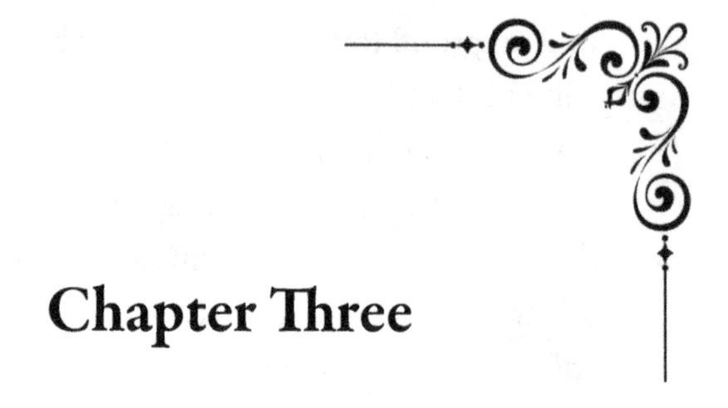

Chapter Three

"I CANNOT BELIEVE I have no choice in the matter," Abigail said while pacing the parlor floor the next morning.

"It's deuced bad luck, I say," her brother, Lance, the Earl of Durham, told her sympathetically while sipping his third cup of coffee. "Although to be fair, you could have landed on someone far less appealing than Mr. James Townsbridge. Just imagine if Viscount Ribbernitting had been lying on that sofa."

Abigail shuddered but managed to say, "At least he has a title. Mama and Papa would have been a lot happier with the prospect of marrying me off to him."

Lance grunted while eyeing her over the rim of his cup. A lock of hazelnut hair matching hers fell forward over his brow. "Townsbridge has always struck me as an affable fellow."

"You don't—"

"He's also terribly handsome."

Muted by the blunt pronouncement spoken from the opposite side of the room, Abigail turned to stare at her sister. Petra might be two years younger than she, but she certainly liked to voice her opinion.

"I thought you were reading," Abigail said.

Petra turned a page in her book with a shrug and without glancing away from the text. "That doesn't mean I can't hear you talking."

"And how would you know what he looks like anyway?" Abigail asked. Her sister wasn't out and hardly ever left the house.

"I have eyes in my head," Petra murmured but added no further explanation.

Sighing, Abigail flopped back against her seat and gazed helplessly up at the ceiling. "Handsome or not, I simply don't like the man." At least not any more.

"You scarcely know him," Lance informed her with the wisdom of an older brother who possessed three more years of life experience than she was able to boast.

Rubbing her brow, she considered his comment. "You're right, of course, but what I do know is that he lacks manners. And that's an integral part of anyone's character, not something that can quickly be acquired. A person is either polite or they're not."

"Like I said," Lance drawled while returning his cup to its saucer, "James Townsbridge has never given me reason to question his behavior."

"Perhaps he was simply having a bad day," Petra offered, "and you became the unfortunate victim of his aggravation."

Abigail twisted her mouth in thought. "I will allow it as a possibility, but only because it makes no sense for him to be so horrid when the rest of his family is nothing but likeable."

"The same could be said about you," Petra muttered, causing Lance to choke on a biscuit he'd just bitten into. He proceeded to cough while Abigail narrowed her eyes on her sister. Only her forehead was visible behind the book.

"What do you mean?"

A pause followed, then Petra snapped the book shut in order to meet her gaze. "Only that you are not as outgoing as we are." She tilted her head. "Are you sure you didn't put Mr. Townsbridge off by looking as though you would rather be elsewhere?"

Abigail flattened her mouth. While it was true she'd always been somewhat shy, this had nothing to do with the anxious unease that had gripped her when she'd realized who her parents meant to introduce her to. "You know I—"

The parlor door opened and Arundel, the butler, appeared. He looked just as stiff and unapproachable as always. "Mr. Tobias Chesterfield has come to call," he said in that dry, acerbic tone only very skilled butlers could pull off without looking daft. Arundel managed to do so with perfection.

"By all means, show him in," Lance said. Arundel departed and Lance met Abigail's gaze. "A pity you turned down *his* offer when he asked."

A snort from the other corner of the room was enough to reveal what Petra thought about that particular comment.

Abigail sighed. "You know perfectly well Papa did so for me." Not that she minded. As a childhood friend of Lance's, Tobias had been a constant part of her life. She liked him and had always felt comfortable in his presence, but marrying him would be downright odd, like putting on your favorite pair of gloves the wrong way around. Not to mention that his name had been touched by scandal, seeing as his brother had fled the country after being accused of embezzlement. Remaining friends with Tobias was one thing. Making him part of the family was quite another.

"I came as soon as I heard," Tobias said after entering the room and greeting everyone. Concern marred his features, creasing his brow and tightening his jaw. He glanced at Lance, then went straight to Abigail and lowered himself to the spot beside her on the sofa. "There is no doubt in my mind that Mr. Townsbridge is a scoundrel who took advantage of you and—"

"The fault is not his alone," Abigail said. Perhaps it was Petra's comment from earlier that had chastened her, perhaps she was simply more awake now and able to think with greater clarity. Or maybe it was the fact that she knew Mr. Townsbridge wasn't the only one to blame for what had happened that caused her to come to his defense. "In fact, if it weren't for my strolling into a dark room and sitting on him, I dare say I wouldn't be in this mess." And neither would Mr. Townsbridge, which made her wonder, for the first time since the calamitous incident occurred, what he must be thinking of her right now. Never mind the rest of his family.

Abigail's toes curled with immediate mortification. Were they having a similar discussion in the Townsbridge House parlor at this exact moment? Had hopeful young ladies vying for Mr. Townsbridge's hand come to sympathize with his plight just as Tobias was doing with her?

The very idea made Abigail jolt to her feet. Tobias stood as well and so did Lance. From her armchair in the corner, Petra watched the proceedings like a spectator at the theatre, eager to know what would happen next.

"That does not excuse him," Tobias said. Concern for her was apparent in his warm and friendly eyes. "If he'd been more careful, you would not have been found in his lap or with part of your gown torn to shreds."

Abigail stared at him, her cheeks flushing with shame as she realized how much the scandal sheets had revealed. "That," her voice trembled slightly at the thought of what all of London Society must be thinking, "was an accident."

"On your part certainly," Tobias said, "though it really doesn't look very good."

"On that we are all agreed," Lance muttered.

"Which is why I would try to improve the appearance of things if I were you," Petra remarked.

Abigail turned to stare at her sister. "Whatever do you mean?"

Petra rolled her eyes. "Make people question what really happened between you and Mr. Townsbridge last night." She stared at Abigail with fierce intensity. "And for God's sake, don't let them think you're cowering in shame."

"Perhaps a walk with me and your siblings in the park would be the thing," Tobias said, his voice both kind and hopeful. "Being seen, showing the world you will not be put out by last night's debacle and that you're actually happy to marry Mr. Townsbridge, could help your reputation tremendously."

Only if she were trying to look like she'd trapped Mr. Townsbridge and felt no remorse whatsoever. Not to mention that being seen with Tobias in public would likely have the opposite result of what she wanted to achieve. But since saying as much was sure to hurt him, she nodded while trying to gather her thoughts.

"Yes," she said. "Hiding away at home will only make matters worse."

"We can go to Gunther's as well," Tobias said with increased excitement.

Lance frowned. He looked both uncomfortable and uncertain. And then Petra opened her mouth, clearly intending to argue this terrible idea, which forced Abigail to say, "As tempting as that sounds, I fear I must decline." She noted the look of disappointed confusion on Tobias's face and swiftly added, "I shall go to Townsbridge House instead and call on my future sisters-in-law."

HALF AN HOUR EARLIER at Townsbridge House

"I'm going to kill Hugh," James grumbled while pacing the length of the parlor floor. "And then I am going to revive him so I can kill him again."

Charles and Bethany watched him from their positions on the sofa. They shared a look – one of those filled with endless paragraphs of unspoken words only a deeply connected couple could manage – and then Charles asked, "Did he hold you captive while forcing brandy down your throat?"

James stopped in the middle of the room and glanced at his feet. The pile in the carpet had been kicked up by the heels of his shoes, leaving a series of crisscrossing tracks behind. "No." He glanced up and met his brother's gaze. "But if Mother had let me stay home and rest instead of insisting I come along to the ball, then I wouldn't be in this situation."

Charles tilted his head. "So then it's Mama's fault?"

Expelling a breath, James pinched the bridge of his nose and slowly shook his head. "No." But he wished it were. He wished he could blame someone besides himself because then there'd at least be a target for his frustration.

Selecting a vacant armchair, he sank down heavily onto the seat. "I have only myself to blame for what happened. And Lady Abigail, of course." He gnashed his teeth just thinking about that awful woman.

"You mustn't judge her too quickly," Bethany said. "In fact, I think you'll find the two of you suit rather well."

James gave his sister-in-law a glare, which earned him a stern look of condemnation from Charles. "I beg your pardon but have you actually met her?"

"On occasion." When James continued to stare at her, Bethany added, "The Marquess and Marchioness of Foxborough have always been close friends of my parents', so I met Abigail often while growing up, though I must confess it's probably three years since I saw her last."

James wasn't surprised. Bethany had been away in America before marrying Charles and since then she'd been busy producing children. With her third one currently on the way, she hadn't attended a social event in at least two months.

"People have been known to change," James pointed out.

Bethany frowned. "Perhaps. But considering the gentle girl with an easy smile and pleasant disposition whom I recall, I cannot quite picture her as the arrogant, sour-faced woman you claim her to be."

"Perhaps you managed to offend her," Charles suggested.

James stared at his brother. "*I* offend *her*?"

"Athena did say you were a bore the entire evening."

James blinked. "It's barely noon. When on earth did you speak with Athena?"

"She stopped by for breakfast to tell us of your engagement," Bethany said. "And according to her, you were not as polite as you should have been when you were introduced to Abigail. In fact, she said you were downright rude, which might explain her stiff response to you and..." She sighed.

"Are you suggesting I am to blame for the way she behaved?" James asked. "Even though she was scowling at me before I said one word to her?"

Bethany pursed her lips. "All I am trying to say is that the two of you clearly got off to a poor start."

He leveled his sister-in-law a steady gaze. "And then she *sat* on me."

"The room was, as I understand it, dark at the time," Bethany said as if trying to visualize what and how the events leading up to James's engagement might have transpired.

"Not so dark that she could not find her way to the sofa," James grumbled. "The fact she did not notice a large shape filling it is mind boggling to say the least."

"As mind boggling as your button tearing her gown?" Charles asked with a smirk.

"That was—" James stopped, paused for a moment, and finally blew out a lengthy breath. "Very well. I will agree Lady Abigail and I share the blame for what happened in that room last night." She more than he, he told himself privately, but nonetheless.

"An excellent observation, dear brother," Charles said.

"But that still doesn't mean I like her," James said before Charles started thinking he might be willing to accept what had happened.

"Perhaps you should try to," Bethany suggested. "After all, you will have to live together."

"Not necessarily," James informed her.

Charles snorted. "You can't remain here and you aren't moving in with us either. And besides, Papa is sacrificing Arlington House just so you and your lovely bride can have a magnificent home of your own. After everything, I dare say he'd take you outside and shoot you himself if you turn your back on that."

James grimaced. "You're right of course. I just—"

"Wish you'd had more say in your own future?"

"Precisely!"

Neither Charles nor Bethany responded to that pronouncement, for which James was grateful. In truth, he felt they'd been churning the matter for too long already. Now it was time to act, and if he were being honest, Bethany's suggestion that he try to make the most of things wasn't the worst. In fact, he'd be less unhappy about all of this if he and Lady Abigail could at least find some way in which to get along. Just enough to make the wedding tolerable.

With this in mind, he stood. "I'm heading out," he said.

Charles straightened and gave his wife a quick glance before asking, "Where to?"

"Why, to call on my betrothed," James said. It took some effort not to regret the decision once he'd made it. Instead, he strode to the door. "If all goes well, I'll find that my first opinion of her was entirely wrong."

Doubtful, he reckoned, but certainly worth praying for.

DETERMINED TO PROVE to all of London, and to herself as well, that marrying James Townsbridge would make her splendidly happy, Abigail made her way along Murray Street with Petra by her side. *I am wrong about him*, she silently chanted. *He is not the rude, obnoxious man I think him to be.* Lance was an excellent judge of character, so if he said James Townsbridge was an amicable gentleman, then that was what he was and she was quite simply wrong about him.

"Abigail." Petra's hand grabbed hold of her arm, causing her to jolt. "Is that not him right now, coming toward us?"

Abigail stopped as if some sort of wall had materialized before her. She stared straight ahead, acknowledged that the handsome man approaching was indeed the very same one to whom she would soon be married, and quickly ducked behind her sister.

"What are you doing?" Petra asked, her voice teetering between annoyance and exasperation.

"What does it look like?" When Abigail had envisioned how calling on Townsbridge House would go, she'd pictured a butler granting her entry to a parlor. Miss Townsbridge and Miss Athena would come to take tea with her. They would discuss something mundane for the sake of smoothing things over, after which Abigail would take her leave. The prospect of seeing Mr. Townsbridge himself had not entered her head at all, allowing her to steady her nerves.

"Being a nitwit?" Petra suggested in answer to her question.

"What is he doing here?" Abigail asked while her stomach began flapping about like a fish out of water. Her own brother never left home before three in the afternoon, and when he finally did, it was by carriage in order to visit his club.

"Taking a walk," Petra replied. She blew out a breath. "I think he's seen us."

"What?" Abigail peeked out from behind Petra's shoulder. And was instantly met by Mr. Townsbridge's censorious scowl. Her flapping stomach did a somersault while her heart started fluttering like a piece of fine linen caught in a breeze.

"Good morning," Mr. Townsbridge said as he came to a halt. His eyes met Abigail's and his frown seemed to deepen, if such a thing were possible. A pause followed, during which he glanced at Petra before returning his gaze to Abigail. He waited for a good three seconds, and then he said, "Ordinarily, you would greet me in return and then introduce me to your companion."

He was right, of course, but that did not entitle him to be so overbearing. Swallowing, Abigail took a step sideways and tried not to think of how queasy she felt. She tried to tamp down her nerves. even though she was trembling from head to toe, and did her best to straighten her spine while raising her chin just enough to suggest she would not be cowed by the likes of him.

Inhaling deeply, she gestured to Petra. "My sister. Lady Petra Bright."

Mr. Townsbridge's dark brown eyes bored into hers, increasing her desire to make a hasty retreat. Instead, she held his gaze until he looked away, giving his attention to Petra instead. "A pleasure," he murmured and touched the brim of his hat.

"Likewise," Petra said with what sounded like a sigh of relief. "I've been very eager to make your acquaintance since learning of my sister's betrothal to you. Congratulations on that, by the way. I have no doubt the two of you will be immensely happy together."

Abigail stared at Petra and so did Mr. Townsbridge. "Indeed," he murmured, after what felt like the most awkward moment ever.

Petra just smiled as if all were as it should be. "We were actually on our way to visit you, if you can believe it," she continued while Abigail began to wish this was all a nightmare from which she would soon awaken.

Mr. Townsbridge raised both eyebrows. "Is that so?"

Abigail cleared her throat and shifted from one foot to the other. "Not you," she managed while clasping her hands together. "Your sisters."

"Ah. Well..." He paused as if considering something, then sighed again. His shoulders sagged and then he said, "As it happens, I was on my way to call on you."

"Oh," Petra said with a beaming smile that put a neat row of white teeth on display. "How serendipitous."

Abigail cringed, dreading what would happen next since it very likely involved Mr. Townsbridge making an awful suggestion like—

"But since we are both out of doors," he said, "perhaps we ought to continue our walks together?"

"But your sisters," Abigail tried, attempting to extricate herself from what promised to be the most trying hour or two of her life.

"We can call on them tomorrow," Petra said.

Abigail turned to her with a glare. "I'll get you for this," she muttered, so low only Petra would hear her. And then Mr. Townsbridge grabbed her by the arm and began leading her away.

WHY DID IT HAVE TO be this particular Bright daughter to whom he'd gotten engaged and not the other? James glanced over his shoulder at Lady Petra, who trailed behind. At least *she* knew how to smile, though he had to admit she looked a bit too young to consider marriage.

Lady Abigail, on the other hand, consisted of shapely curves and the sort of kissable lips most men would dream of in a woman. A pity all of this was ruined by her ill-tempered disposition. And yet, there was nothing for it but to make the best of the situation since, as Charles had already pointed out, he was stuck with this woman for better or worse.

With that in mind, James decided to make an attempt at small talk by commenting on the weather. "We're lucky it isn't raining," were the first brilliant words to leave his mouth.

As expected, Her Haughtiness responded with a thin smile and a nod.

Well, James decided, he wasn't going to walk in utter silence, so if she wouldn't speak, he would, whether she liked it or not. "If it were raining, you see, we'd be much worse off than we already are," he went on without knowing where these words strung together would lead. "Although, getting drenched might be a welcome distraction, don't you think?"

He hadn't expected an answer, so he was surprised when she turned her head sideways, as if addressing the street, and muttered, "It would if we were to catch our deaths."

Surely he'd misheard her. "I beg your pardon?"

"What?"

He frowned at her and caught a flicker of something curious in her eyes before she averted her gaze once more. He also saw her blush – a deep crimson hue creeping into her cheeks.

"Well," he said, "I suppose some of the guests would be disappointed if that were to happen. Especially those from your side of the family. But at least the vicar won't mind."

At some point while he'd been talking, she'd focused her eyes more fully upon him, forcing him to acknowledge that they were the most perfect shade of blue he'd ever encountered. They weren't the washed-out hue he'd seen so often before, but a far more solid color that reminded him of forget-me-nots.

"The vicar?" she asked, as if unsure whether or not pursuing this issue further was wise.

"Well, he'll still have a service to perform either way, so—"

A snort, the most indelicate one he'd ever heard, travelled up Lady Abigail's throat in a croaking and grunting sort of way. The color in her cheeks deepened and her face contorted into something that looked almost painful.

And in that moment, James realized Lady Abigail had an intriguing sense of humor. He also learned that she wasn't accustomed to laughing. At least not in public. In fact, upon further reflection, it occurred to him that she looked incredibly uncomfortable. And then the oddest thing happened. She simply trained her features, like a school mistress putting her students in line, until every trace of amusement had vanished.

But James wasn't going to accept her aloof demeanor anymore. Not when she'd just revealed there was more to her than met the eye.

So he drew her slightly closer and leaned in to whisper next to her ear. "Whatever your reason for acting as though you detest everything, I mean to discover it." She inhaled sharply, which gave him the satisfaction of knowing she was indeed hiding something. "Of course, you could simply tell me about it right now."

They entered the park and were instantly met by curious gazes from those who knew them. James smiled and nodded by way of greeting in order to try and convey the outward appearance of a man enamored, instead of one heading for the gallows.

"No," she said, so softly he scarcely heard her above the sound of a carriage's wheels crunching the gravel as it rolled past.

That was all. Just one word and not a very helpful one at that.

James frowned. He'd been doing a lot of that since making her acquaintance last night. Glancing at her, he noted her free hand was now pressed to her belly and that she was taking deep breaths. "Are you unwell?" he asked. If so, it would explain a great deal.

She looked at him in surprise and then quickly nodded. "Yes. I believe so." The delicate lines in her neck moved as she swallowed. "Must be something I ate."

He felt his frown deepen. "Then I must apologize to you, my lady, for I was not aware. You should have said something when I suggested the walk."

"I tried."

"By insisting you call on my sisters!" What the devil was wrong with this woman?

"It seemed like the right thing to do," she muttered.

James blinked. While logic compelled him to shake her for such a misguided idea, something inside James softened in response to her wanting to make things better. Deciding that chastising her wouldn't help at this point, he drew her to a halt and turned to face her, then gently asked, "Did you by any chance happen to eat the same thing today as yesterday?"

Her eyes widened for a second before clouding over with hesitation. "Perhaps. I don't know. It's possible, I suppose." The words were spoken in a rush, as if she were somehow afraid to acknowledge them.

Clearly, she found the subject embarrassing, but it was a necessary one, James decided. So he ignored Lady Petra, who'd now caught up with them, and told Lady Abigail plainly, "I think you ought to consider the possibility that there is a food that does not agree with you."

"I...um..."

"Is something the matter?" Lady Petra asked, looking from James to Lady Abigail and back at him again with interest.

James glared at her. She was Lady Abigail's sister, for God's sake. How could she not have noticed that something was wrong? In fact, upon further observation, James decided that Lady Abigail looked rather pale.

"Your sister is feeling poorly," he told Lady Petra. A thought struck him – one he had not considered until this moment because he'd been too annoyed and self-absorbed and utterly convinced she had wronged him by being a fool. But there was another explanation for why she'd been in that parlor last night and why she'd not noticed him there. "Were you trying to escape the ballroom last night because you felt ill?"

Lady Abigail nodded. "I'm sorry," she said. "My stomach—"

"Please," James hastened to say. "You need not apologize when I was there for much the same reason as you. My head, you see, was in tremendous pain. So much so I would not have noticed you either if you'd been the one on the sofa."

"I...I had no idea," Lady Abigail said, her expression easing a little in response to his confession.

"Neither did I." He turned to Lady Petra. "I think the best course of action right now is for you to take your sister home. She clearly needs rest."

Lady Petra raised an eyebrow, but rather than argue as he feared she might be about to do, she nodded. "Of course."

"And have a word with your cook," James said. He met Lady Abigail's gaze. "I'd like to get to the bottom of this so you can start feeling better."

Lady Abigail took a deep breath. "Thank you."

James nodded. "I'll call on you in a couple of days to see how you're doing." And then he took his leave, walking one way while Lady Abigail and her sister went another. By the time he returned home he'd decided he was an imbecile. He'd completely misjudged the woman with whom he was destined to spend the rest of his life, and it was time for him to right that wrong.

Chapter Four

IT WAS ALMOST A WEEK since Abigail had last seen Mr. Townsbridge, a day she recalled as the one where he'd proven he had a good reason for being ill-tempered the night they'd met, and the one where she'd proven herself a liar. It had been wrong of her to mislead him – even Petra had disapproved – but when he'd inquired about her wellbeing, blaming her ailment on something she'd eaten had seemed so much simpler than telling the truth.

Because really, how did one inform a man that he was responsible for her fluttering heart, the reason she feared casting up her accounts, and why she could never think of what to say while in his presence? It was impossible to do so.

And so she'd dreaded having to see him again. For she'd known her palms would start sweating, her legs turn to jelly, and her brain to mush the moment she did. But contrary to what he'd told her when they'd parted ways in the park, he hadn't come to call in the days that followed. Instead, he'd sent a letter, excusing himself until further notice and inquiring about her health.

And since writing a letter was simple enough and something she actually excelled at, Abigail had responded, informing him that her health was much improved. She'd added a few extra points about the wedding preparations, signed it, and paused. For long moments after, she'd stared at the piece of paper and then, recklessly, she'd added: *P.S. I am also planning a funeral. Just in case.*

A day had gone by without a response, during which she'd started to fear that she'd gone too far. She'd even begun wondering if there were a way for her to retrieve the blasted letter and tear it to shreds before he read it. Perhaps she'd misread him when he'd made that comment about the vicar. Perhaps he hadn't been joking. In which case he must think something was wrong with her for responding as she had, as if what he'd said was incredibly funny.

But then, when she'd just about convinced herself that her only viable option was to leave the country and never return, she'd received another letter from him, this one slightly longer than the last and with a post script of his own which read: *If you would be kind enough to tell me your height, I can order the caskets.*

A smile had spread across her face, replacing all doubt with joy. And then she'd laughed. Not only because of his perfect response but because it had given her hope. If she could just get her nerves under control where he was concerned, then there was a chance of things turning out well between them.

Additional letters had followed, during which Abigail had become increasingly certain that when she met Mr. Townsbridge again, she would be able to speak with him properly. She even fantasized about what she would say and how he'd respond, about sharing smiles and laughter, and slowly falling in love.

Until she arrived at Bethany Townsbridge's home for dinner one evening and realized fantasy was very different from reality. Because the moment she followed her parents into the parlor and actually saw him, her heart leapt into her throat and her stomach began turning inside out. His eyes, fixed solely on her, seemed brighter than ever before. And then he smiled, the sort of smile that spoke of shared secrets and something bordering on sin.

Abigail felt the familiar queasiness swamp her. She took a deep breath and attempted a smile of her own, only to find that it felt too tight.

Abigail's parents, Miranda and Edward, wasted no time in greeting Bethany and her husband, Charles Townsbridge. Abigail followed suit and even managed to address Viscount and Viscountess Roxley, her soon-to-be parents-in-law with a polite, "How do you do?"

But when she was faced with James Townsbridge himself, the air seemed to thicken, making it harder to breathe. She tried to inhale, to force her quickening heartbeats into a calmer rhythm. But it was to no avail. The effect he had on her was so intense, she started to fear her knees might buckle beneath her weight.

He frowned at her. "You do not look well," he said while searching her face in a way that only increased her discomfort. "Based on our correspondence, I imagined you'd found the source of your malaise, but that's clearly not the case."

"I...um..." Oh, how she wished she could get both her mind and body under control. Instead she just stood there, unable speak.

"Fresh air," Mr. Townsbridge declared as if stumbling upon some fantastic discovery. Before Abigail could blink, he'd linked his arm with hers and steered her through to an adjoining sitting room. "We're going for a walk," he added while passing his brother.

"But dinner's about to be served," Charles Townsbridge said.

"Then you must excuse us," James Townsbridge told him without breaking his stride. "Lady Abigail is in need of fresh air, which I intend to provide. We shall return as soon as she's feeling better."

"Thank you," Abigail murmured as soon as they'd exited onto the terrace and she'd managed to take a deep breath. The air was cool and fresh, infused with the sweet scent of jasmine growing nearby.

Mr. Townsbridge released her arm and strolled along the terrace for a number of paces before turning to face her. "What have you eaten today?"

Abigail stared at him. His features were harder to read now due to the darkness obscuring his face, but his tone was firm and very determined.

Pretending interest in the garden, Abigail turned away, allowing herself to believe he wasn't there and she was alone. Which instantly settled her stomach and calmed her nerves. "I had toast with butter and jam for breakfast, minced meat pie for luncheon and some grapes for my afternoon snack." She closed her eyes, aware it was time to be honest. Inhaling, she forced herself to say, "But the truth is—"

"Did you also eat all of these things on the days you were feeling well?"

Instinctively she shook her head. "I'm not sure, but—"

"Try to think. Perhaps you have an intolerance toward something used in the pie or...which fruit was the jam made from? I've heard strawberries can have a negative effect on some people."

"It isn't the strawberries. It is..." He said nothing else, allowing silence to gather around her. Three words, that was all it would take to make him see, and as much as she wished she could walk away and never discuss this subject again, she knew she had to face it, for both their sakes. So she straightened her spine, drew back her shoulders, and leapt into the awaiting abyss.

"It is you," she said quickly, before she had time to change her mind.

JAMES STARED AT HIS bride-to-be and tried to absorb the meaning behind the words she'd just spoken. "Am I to understand," he asked her slowly, "that you feel sick because of me?"

She spun toward him. "It is not..." Her words scattered the moment her eyes met his.

"It is not what?" James pressed with growing irritation. He wasn't sure what annoyed him more, the fact that she'd made him believe she suffered from some food related illness or that he'd enjoyed their recent correspondence so much he'd actually looked forward to seeing her again.

"It is not as bad as you think."

He stared at her. "I hope you'll explain what you mean by that because frankly, from my point of view, few things are worse than learning I can have such a negative effect on someone." Devil take it, he was tempted to leave her out here, excuse himself to the rest of the party, and escape to his club for the rest of the evening.

"It is just that," she began, only to stop midsentence. She shifted from foot to foot, then dropped her gaze and mumbled something James couldn't hear.

He moved toward her, his curiosity overpowering his annoyance.

Her chin jerked up, perhaps in response to his approaching footsteps. The gasp she emitted was accompanied by a pair of wide eyes. And then she took a step back, like a startled filly preparing to flee.

"For God's sake," James muttered, his irritation with her returning tenfold. "I thought we were starting to get along. Based on the letters we exchanged, I even believed we shared the same odd sense of humor. But I am beginning to wonder if you wrote those letters yourself, for I swear you're not the same person who made me believe that marrying you might not be so bad after all. But of course, that was before I realized you misled me."

"I didn't mean to," she said.

"Then explain why you didn't correct my misconception. The opportunity to do so was there, in one of the three letters you wrote to me this past week."

There was a slight tremor to her voice when she responded with, "I'm sorry."

Stupidly, he felt compelled to go to her and tell her it was all right. Except it wasn't all right, and he would not be the sort of fool who allowed a woman to deal him the worst sort of blow to his masculine pride, only to help her feel better about having done so.

"So am I," he told her crisply. He'd let himself get carried away by a fantasy. "Shall we go back inside?"

For a moment she looked like she might say no, but then she nodded, turned away, and preceded him through the French doors. Thankfully, the seating arrangement at the dinner table was such that James managed to avoid conversing with her for the remainder of the evening. When it was finally time for her and her parents to depart, he said the bare minimum since saying more would likely have ended badly.

"You were in a mood this evening," Charles remarked once the Brights had departed. He and James had stepped into the foyer to see them off while Bethany remained in the parlor with their parents.

"I'm just not thrilled with the idea of tying myself to Lady Abigail for the rest of my life," James grumbled. In fact, knowing he repulsed her made him both grumpy and depressed.

Charles shoved his hands in his trouser pockets and gave James a sympathetic smile. "I'll agree she seemed a little standoffish, but she wasn't rude, which I think suggests she must be shy. If you can find a way to break her out of her shell, the two of you might get along quite well."

Deciding not to share what Lady Abigail had told him out on the terrace, James simply nodded. "You're probably right."

"Don't forget that she and Bethany are friends," Charles added. "And Bethany has only positive things to say about her."

James had to admit Charles was right, though he couldn't quite fathom the reality of it. Bethany was fun and vibrant while Abigail came across as the direct opposite. But then again, that might only be when *he* was around.

Allowing an inward groan, James followed his brother back into the parlor. The conversation that had been taking place between his parents and Bethany died as soon as he entered.

A moment of awkward silence followed, and then his mother said, "You really must make more of an effort, James. Why, you hardly spoke more than two words to your poor fiancée all evening. It's no wonder she looked so unhappy."

"You neglected her," Roxley added in that dry tone he used to reprimand. "I dare say your manners were utterly lacking."

James stared at them all in turn while trying to figure out how to respond without sounding horribly rude. Eventually he said, "We spoke at length while we were taking some air on the terrace."

"About what?" his mother demanded.

Since being completely honest would only lead to comments and questions he had no interest in facing, he said, "Our likes and dislikes."

"Did she mention charades?" Bethany asked. When James shook his head, his sister-in-law knit her brow. "How odd. It used to be one of her favorite games."

James struggled to hold back a snort. He could not for the life of him envision Lady Abigail engaging in such an outgoing activity. "Perhaps it's not anymore. After all, people do change and it has been some years since you saw her last."

"I suppose," Bethany conceded though she didn't look even remotely convinced.

"What does she like then, if not charades?" Charles asked. He'd taken a seat next to his wife while James remained standing.

James opened his mouth and uttered an uncertain, "Umm..." which led to some very perplexed expressions until he was able to gather his thoughts and say, "Playing pretend."

His father tilted his head and gave him a rather odd look. "Is that not the same as charades?"

"Not exactly," James murmured. It involved trapping unsuspecting men into marriage and then deceiving them so completely they started to imagine there was hope for the future.

"Well," his mother remarked, "that's hardly any information at all. Certainly not very useful." She expelled a suffering breath. "Really, James, you must do better. Which is why I suggest you call on Lady Abigail tomorrow. Bring her some flowers and try to... James? Are you listening?"

He was. But the idea of having to spend time with Lady Abigail again so soon had practically paralyzed him.

"Honestly," his mother continued, "I dare say this is part of the problem. Women like to be heard, James. So please, encourage Lady Abigail to speak, and do your best to listen to what she has to say."

"Or at the very least, pretend to," Roxley said. "That's what I do most of the time."

This comment earned the viscount a slap on his arm from his wife, though it was accompanied by a mischievous smile. The two shared a look – the sort that suggested they were both enjoying a private joke.

James sank onto a vacant chair with a sigh. This was the kind of relationship he wanted for himself. Why the devil did it have to be so hard to obtain?

HAVING VENTURED INTO the garden the following day after breakfast, Abigail chose to pass the morning by deadheading the roses, an activity she found both relaxing and rewarding. It also kept her mind off the previous evening and, most importantly, away from a certain Mr. Townsbridge. Good heavens, she still could not fathom how rude she had been. Of course, it hadn't been her intention to make him think he made her ill, but her inability to explain herself properly had caused him to do precisely that. Which only made her more nervous about seeing him again and...

"There you are," came Tobias's voice.

Abigail looked up and waved when she saw her brother's friend striding across the grass. "I'm afraid Lance has gone out," she said.

"So I've been told. But since you're here, I thought I'd see you instead. I told Arundel I'd manage to find you myself."

"And so you have," she said with a grin. Setting the knife she'd been using aside in a nearby basket, she went to greet him. "Would you care for some tea? Or perhaps some refreshing lemonade?"

"Arundel already offered. Some lemonade should be on its way along with a plate of biscuits." Together, they made their way up to the terrace where a wrought iron table and chairs stood beneath the shade of a nearby birch. "How are your wedding preparations coming along?" Tobias asked once they were both comfortably seated.

"Can we not find another subject to discuss?"

"That bad, is it?"

A maid brought a tray with refreshments which she placed on the table. Glasses were filled and Abigail took a quick sip of her tart drink before saying, "I may have suggested to Mr. Townsbridge that I feel unwell in his company."

Tobias responded with a guffaw that ended in a half-choked cough. His eyes went wide. "You did not." When she nodded, he laughed even more. "Good God, Abby. Whatever were you thinking?"

She shrugged. "I was just trying to be honest."

He stared at her. "How so?"

"It's nothing." Confiding in Tobias was probably a mistake. "Forget I said anything."

This just made him frown. And then he reached for her hand. "Abby, if Mr. Townsbridge has treated you ill in some way, then I would suggest you speak up now before it's too late."

"I—"

Her words were cut short by the unexpected arrival of the man they had just been discussing. James Townsbridge was suddenly there, his expression utterly grave as he looked straight at her. "Good morning, my lady." His gaze dropped to her hand and she hastily pulled it away from Tobias's. The edge of Mr. Townsbridge's mouth twitched. "I hope I'm not imposing too much."

Abigail's silly heart fluttered madly against her breast. Her stomach did that annoying flip it always did when she was faced with the handsomest man in existence. She swallowed, attempted to speak, but then changed her mind and just shook her head.

"Arundel ought to have brought Mr. Townsbridge's card first," Tobias told Abigail. His visible displeasure almost made her remind him that the aging butler hadn't detained him either.

But she lost her chance when Mr. Townsbridge said, "He knows I'm about to be part of this family." The words, *unlike you*, were heavily implied. "And then Lady Roxley arrived in the foyer, and she agreed that it would be fine for me to come find you myself, seeing as you already have company." He sat and placed a bouquet of roses on the table. "These are for you."

"Th...thank you," Abigail managed.

Mr. Townsbridge responded with a glower. And then he said, "Now, if you don't mind, Mr. Chesterfield, I would like to have a private conversation with my future wife."

"Only if the lady agrees," Tobias said. He made no hint of planning to get up anytime soon.

"She does," Mr. Townsbridge clipped. His voice sounded increasingly angry.

Abigail forced herself not to look at him and to focus on Tobias instead. In doing so, she was able to calm her nerves a little. "It's all right." She managed a smile. "I'm sure Mr. Townsbridge and I have much to discuss. Thank you so much for coming to visit and...for your concern."

"Think nothing of it." Tobias hesitated briefly, then stood. Rounding the table, he placed one hand on Abigail's shoulder. "Perhaps I should ask one of the maids to come chaperone?"

"You required no such thing," Mr. Townsbridge pointed out.

Tobias calmly told him, "Abby has known me most of her life. More importantly though, I do not make her feel uneasy."

For a second, it looked like Mr. Townsbridge might grab the bouquet he'd brought and use it to give Tobias a thrashing. But then he said, "A misunderstanding, I believe, and the reason why I am here." This remark was followed by a pointed look that gave Tobias no other choice but to take his leave.

Silence fell, thick and uncomfortable, and then a maid arrived. She placed a clean glass on the table for Mr. Townsbridge and then removed herself to a nearby bench.

Mr. Townsbridge snorted and rolled his eyes. "Abby?"

"He...um..." She took a deep breath and prayed she'd be able to speak a full sentence without her words sticking together. "Toby...I mean, Mr. Chesterfield and I—"

"Are you in love with him?"

"What?"

"Well, he's clearly in love with you, so it is a reasonable question for me to ask."

"I...um..." While it was true Tobias had offered for her hand, he'd never declared having feelings for her that went beyond the bounds of friendship. So she'd assumed he'd done it because he thought it might be expected, and because he'd been hoping her family wouldn't dismiss him based on his brother's actions. Of course, he'd been wrong. She was a marquess's daughter and appearances mattered.

Mr. Townsbridge grunted. "Unfortunately, I am the man you'll be marrying, so you should probably try to tolerate my company. No matter how sick that makes you."

JAMES HAD ARRIVED AT Roxley House with the best of intentions. He'd put a great deal of thought into the bouquet he'd purchased, eventually settling on a particular shade of pink roses matching the gown Lady Abigail had worn the previous evening. But when he'd reached the doors leading to the garden, the sound of masculine laughter coming from the terrace had made him stop and listen.

"Good God, Abby," sputtered a man he'd soon discover to be Mr. Chesterfield. "Whatever were you thinking?"

"I was just trying to be honest," Lady Abigail replied.

A pause had followed before Mr. Chesterfield asked, "How so?"

"It's nothing." Lady Abigail had spoken so low James had struggled to hear the words. "Forget I said anything."

Understanding Mr. Chesterfield's emphatic response, however, had not been difficult. The man had spoken clearly and with extreme passion when he'd said, "Abby, if Mr. Townsbridge has treated you ill in some way, then I would suggest you speak up now before it's too late."

The nerve of the man to suggest such a thing! Incensed, James had made his presence known only to find the blighter holding Lady Abigail's hand. At which point James had abandoned every intention he'd had of trying to be polite. It didn't matter if he didn't like her much himself. Somehow, seeing another man showing an interest made him possessive and downright boorish.

Which probably explained his inability to say something nice to the woman with whom he would soon face a vicar. Her cheeks had turned a delightful shade of pink, not that he cared.

And she was eyeing him carefully from beneath her lashes, as if looking at him directly required extreme caution.

He, on the other hand, was determined to be direct. "I'm sorry on both our behalves that we must marry. You may rest assured that if I could somehow prevent it from happening, I would." Her eyes widened and started to shimmer, which made no sense at all. After all, she was the one who had said she couldn't tolerate him. And yet...a tear now slid down her cheek.

James's chest grew suddenly tight. He tried to think of what to say, but before he managed to do so, Lady Abigail had risen and walked away. He stared after her as she stepped down onto the grass and walked toward a flowerbed filled with roses. As she went, she dismissed the maid, who quickly disappeared back into the house.

Puzzled and unsure of what to do, James stood and glanced around. On one hand, he was tempted to leave and avoid further conversation, but on the other, he was curious to know what was going on. Lady Abigail's response to his proclamation was downright bizarre if she felt the same way as him about the wedding, which he'd been certain she did in light of what she'd told him.

Raising his eyes to the sky, he blew out a breath before striding after her. With two sisters, one would think he'd have some understanding of women by now, but either he didn't or this one was simply proving to be particularly complex.

Having passed the roses, she was now moving along a graveled path that led to a boxed-in corner where neatly trimmed hedges offered a private spot no doubt intended for contemplation. Four stone benches stood there, but Lady

Abigail chose not to sit. Instead she remained standing, her back toward him as he approached.

"Stop. Please...don't come any closer." Her voice was soft but firm, prompting him to comply.

Before this moment, he would have taken offense at her wish to avoid his company. But now...

As he stood there studying her, he noticed something tortured about her entire person. It was almost as if she were carrying some colossal weight upon her shoulders. And then, of course, there was the tear.

"Lady Abigail." She seemed to flinch a little in response to his voice, so he paused briefly before asking, "Is something the matter?" When she failed to respond, he gently added, "I'm sorry for what I said about not wanting to marry you. But after what you told me last night and then seeing Mr. Chesterfield treat you with such familiarity, I just—"

"Please." Her voice cracked beneath that one word. "I..." She drew a shuddering breath. "I am the one who owes you an apology. For not expressing myself properly."

She was speaking to the hedge, James noted, and yet this was the most she'd ever said while in his company. "You could do so now," he suggested. The gravel crunched beneath his feet as he took a step forward.

Lady Abigail gasped. "Only if you stay where you are. Please. I cannot function properly when you are near."

Trying not to feel affronted, James halted his progress and did as she asked. Glancing sideways, he considered the opposite side of the hedge from where she stood and crossed to that spot instead. "Very well," he told her when she was no longer within his line of vision. "You can turn around if you wish without having to see me. And when you're ready, I'll listen to whatever it is you would like to say."

Chapter Five

ABIGAIL KNEW SHE WAS the biggest dunderhead to ever walk the earth. She didn't dare think what Mr. Townsbridge's opinion was of her at this moment. But she appreciated his willingness to comply with what must seem like a very strange wish indeed. Out of sight and completely silent, he gave the impression of not being there at all, which bolstered her courage.

"When I told you that you are to blame for my feeling unwell, I neglected to let you know why." Her stomach did a quick flutter that always preceded a nervous panic, so she took a moment to tamp down the crippling sensation and then said, "The truth of the matter is I have admired you for some time. At least three years, if you really must know. And while I will confess to being disappointed when I finally met you, all of that changed after you told me about your headache.

"And now that I've gotten to know you better, I find that I really like you. A lot. So much, in fact, my heart starts pounding harder than ever before when I see you, my legs begin to tremble, and my stomach rolls over." She paused in case he wished to respond, but when he didn't, she continued, pretending only the garden was listening. "Every time I try to speak to you, my throat closes up and the words jam together.

But the biggest problem of all is the nausea, for it makes me feel horribly unwell, not because you repel me but rather because of how handsome you are. I just..." She breathed a heavy sigh. "I've never felt like this with anyone else, so it caught me rather by surprise. But the fact of the matter is I think you're wonderful. It's just that my nerves, you see... They make it quite impossible for me to be around you without turning into an anxious ninny."

There. She'd said more to him than she'd meant to and there was no going back. He'd either roll his eyes and call her a blockhead or make an attempt at helping her find a way through this. When she reckoned five minutes had passed without him saying a word, she started to wonder if he might have walked away during her speech.

She was about to call his name and ask him to share his opinion (if he was still there), when he said, "I'm just a man, Abby."

Abby.

Only her family and closest friends had ever called her that. She liked hearing Mr. Townsbridge do so, for it conveyed a degree of intimacy between them that made her feel more at ease.

Although...

"That's the thing," she said in answer to his comment. "You're not just a man. You're...You're the most attractive man I've ever known and... Oh blast!" She heard a distinct snort from behind the hedge and rushed to offer an apology.

"No need," he hastened to say. "In fact, I find this side of you quite refreshing."

That made her smile. "You like women who curse and have morbid senses of humor?"

"I like you," he said, "when you're being yourself."

"A pity it's only possible for me to do so with you via writing or with a hedge placed between us."

There was a pause, and then, "Close your eyes, Abby."

"Why?"

"Because I want to try something."

"Mr. Townsbridge, I—"

"You really should call me James."

Her pulse leapt in response to his smooth tone. "Very well, James."

"That's better." He paused, then asked, "Are your eyes closed now?"

She nodded, then recalled that he wouldn't be able to see her doing so and said, "Yes."

"Good. Because unless you plan to keep a constant barrier between us or only to speak with me in writing, we need to tackle your nerves and bring them to heel. After all, I would like to kiss you."

Her eyes flew open and he was suddenly there, just inches away. Somehow, while he'd been talking, distracting her with his words, she'd missed the fact that he'd been approaching.

"Shh... Easy does it," he murmured when she took a step back. "Close your eyes again so you don't have to look at me. We'll work through this together, all right?"

Sucking in a deep breath, Abigail did as he asked and nodded. The queasiness that usually overcame her when he was near had started to rise the moment she'd seen him right before her. So she took another series of breaths and tried to ignore it.

"You're feeling ill again, aren't you?"

"I'm so sorry, I just—"

"Don't be. Now that I know why this is happening, there's no need for you to apologize." His comment was followed by the gentle touch of his palm against her cheek. It was wonderfully warm and inviting, and she found herself leaning against it without even thinking. "You should know that I also find you incredibly attractive."

Abigail's face grew unbearably hot and her heart started skipping around as if not quite sure of where it belonged. But then she felt the soft press of James's lips against hers, and all her focus went to that point of sensual contact. She forgot who she was and where she was. Every uncertainty she felt in his company was swept away by this new kind of touch, and all she could do was feel.

His free hand moved to her back, settling firmly against the base of her spine and holding her steady. The other continued to cup her cheek while angling her head just so. The scent of him, a combination of sandalwood and bergamot, filled the air around her.

Needing to steady herself in the face of the heady experience, she wound her arms around his neck, bringing herself flush against his solid chest.

A low groan of pure satisfaction rose from his throat, stirring to life a series of new sensations inside her. Gone were the awkward nervousness and the dreaded fear she might cast up her accounts at any second. In their place was an eager need to explore this new experience to its fullest. So she didn't draw away when he deepened the kiss, nor when he pulled her more firmly against him. Instead, she started to wish he'd do something more, though she wasn't quite sure what that "something more" should be.

GOD, HOW HE WANTED her. The way she responded as he kissed her proved what she'd told him was true. It wasn't an aversion toward him that made her act strange, but rather a burning desire, the likes of which he'd never known before. She'd claimed an attraction, but this was far more than that. This...this was a force that would bind them together forever and make sure they had no trouble at all in the bedroom. Hell, he was ready to lift up her skirts right now and take her against the hedge he was so bloody mad for her.

The confession she'd made and the courage it must have taken to make it only compounded his need to claim her. Which was rather odd in a way, when considering how frustrated and angry she'd made him not so long ago.

His hand crept down over her bottom so he could secure her more firmly against him. Christ, that felt good! And the sigh she emitted...

He kissed her harder, releasing all of the aggravation she'd caused him, while relishing the new turn their relationship had taken. If they could maintain this degree of wild passion, they'd be all right for decades to come. But since claiming her innocence here in her parents' garden would be utterly reprehensible, he carefully, gently, and most regrettably, eased her away and took a step back.

Cheeks flushed and with her hair in slight disarray, she stood with her eyes still closed, looking wonderfully ravished.

For a few long seconds, all James could do was stare at her, this lovely impassioned woman who'd soon be his wife.

"That was," he finally managed while sounding as though he'd just raced up a hill, "sensational."

A shy smile pulled at her lips. "I must confess, I've never experienced anything quite like it."

"I should certainly hope not," he muttered.

In response to which she opened her eyes and looked at him, not with unease this time, but with absolute clarity and...something he reckoned was a mixture of happiness and yearning. "You taste incredible."

Her remark was so unexpected, James couldn't stop from laughing even as he felt his own cheeks grow warm. Hell, he'd never been one to blush and yet he was doing so now. "So do you," he said when he noted the wariness in her eyes. Now that she'd started relaxing around him, he'd fight to keep her from going back inside her shell.

"I have the oddest desire to touch you right now," she confessed after a moment of silence. "Is that normal?"

James coughed and made a stoic attempt not to conjure up all sorts of wonderful ways in which her hands might please him. "Um. Yes." He cleared his throat. "I want to touch you as well." Everywhere. While they both wore fewer clothes.

Her smile widened. And then, confirming that her mind was not as filthy as his, she held out her hand for him to take. "Thank you for helping me banish my nerves," she said as they walked back toward the terrace. "My stomach's still somewhat uneasy, but it's nowhere near as bad as it was before."

"I'm glad." He squeezed her hand. "And Abby, I want you to try and be honest with me from now on. No matter how hard it may be at times, confronting the truth as quickly as possible can prevent misunderstandings and save us days' worth of aggravation."

"You're right." She glanced at him and blushed. "I've been very silly, I know."

"A little," he conceded, "but now that I realize it's because of how gorgeous I am, I really can't blame you."

She slapped his arm and laughed, the delightful sound lifting his heart and causing his spirit to soar. Because now he was certain he and Abby would be wonderfully happy together. And nothing was going to change that.

THE NEXT WEEK AND A half before the wedding passed in a blur. Abigail kept busy with the fitting of her wedding gown, the preparation of her trousseau, or some other wedding-related chore. In between it all, she spent as much time with James as possible, going for walks, having ices at Gunther's, visiting museums, and simply getting to know him better. Unfortunately, they'd been alone only two times since that magical day in the garden, which meant they'd had only two chances of sharing additional kisses. Much to Abigail's disappointment.

"How are the preparations at Arlington House coming along?" she asked James a couple of days before the wedding while walking with him in Hyde Park. It was a muggy day and she'd woken to it with a blistering headache that dampened her mood. When James had come to call and she'd told him she wouldn't be very good company, he'd insisted she get some exercise and a bit of fresh air.

"Better now that I'm looking forward to my wedding night." The wicked gleam in James's eyes as he spoke caused her cheeks to grow hot. Grinning with rakish abandon, he tucked her hand more securely against the crook of his arm. "I do so love how easy it is for me to affect you."

A stabbing pain pierced Abigail's skull at that exact moment. She winced, which caused James to frown. "Are you all right?"

"No. No I'm not," she grumbled.

"Hmm." They walked a few more paces before he said, "In answer to your question, I've asked Mrs. Anderson, the housekeeper, to replace some of the carpets and a few faded curtains. The entire building felt stuffy when I went to visit a few days ago so it's also being aired out. As for the rest of the things that need doing..." He shrugged. "I thought it might be nice to do them together so you're included in the decisions."

Abigail wanted to smile. Indeed, she tried to do so but ended up squeezing her eyes shut instead. "That's very thoughtful," she said and took a deep breath. "I really—"

"Abby!"

Her name, spoken so loudly it jarred her brain, forced a groan from between her clenched teeth. Recognizing the voice, she turned to find Tobias striding toward her. He'd called on her repeatedly this past week, but she'd either been out with James or otherwise occupied by wedding preparations and unable to see him.

Frowning, he drew to a halt before her. "Good afternoon." Eyes trained on her, he barely acknowledging James with, "Townsbridge."

James gave a curt nod in return.

Abigail sighed, causing Tobias's frown to deepen. "You don't look well, Abby."

At her side, she felt James stiffen in response to Tobias's familiar form of address. "Her head is paining her today."

Tobias glared at James. "Are you certain that's all that's the matter?"

"I don't really care for your tone," James told him. "Or what you are implying."

Muttering something beneath his breath, Tobias returned his attention to Abigail. Concern was evident in his eyes. "I'm worried about you."

"You needn't be," Abigail said. Her voice sounded weaker than she would have liked. "Everything is fine. In fact, I couldn't be happier."

Tobias gave her an odd look. "Are you sure?"

"Yes, she's sure," James said, his patience apparently wearing thin. "Now, if you'll please excuse us, Mr. Chesterfield, we really must get going if we're to return to Foxborough House in time for tea." He gave Abigail's arm a gentle tug.

"Perhaps I should walk with you," Tobias suggested.

Fearing what James might say in response to that suggestion, Abigail hastened to say, "Thank you for the offer, Toby—" James's arm went rigid "—but Mr. Townsbridge and I have a few things we need to discuss before the wedding."

Tobias did not look pleased, but he relented nonetheless. "Very well then. I shall call on you tomorrow."

"The devil you will," James muttered so low that Abigail knew only she could have heard him. He tipped his hat politely and steered her away from Tobias. When they'd gone a few paces he told her plainly, "I cannot abide that man."

Abigail sighed. "He's just being protective of me."

"Because he's in love with you," James growled.

She couldn't help but smile in response to his possessive tone, no matter how much her head hurt. "You needn't be jealous."

"Jealous? Ha! Of all the preposterous things to suggest."

A low chuckle escaped her, causing another jolt of pain. Abigail did her best to relax her features. "Either way, Toby's feelings—"

"Would you please stop calling him that!"

"Fine." Abigail hadn't wanted to get annoyed with James, but his overbearingness coupled with her headache was starting to be an unbearable burden. "Mr. *Chesterfield's* feelings hardly matter since I am not in love with him."

"It matters when he's making eyes at my fiancée in public," James grumbled.

"Honestly, I think you're imagining something that isn't there."

"Am not!"

She shot him a look that she hoped would inform him of just how childish she thought he was being. "You are the man I want to marry. Isn't that enough?"

He glanced at her and finally smiled. "Of course it is." Raising her hand to his lips, he placed a kiss upon her gloved knuckles.

"So then you'll agree to forget about everyone else and just focus on the two of us?"

"Your wish is my command," James assured her.

His answer lifted her spirits and banished all her concerns.

FOR THE NEXT TWO DAYS, James did his best to put the uncomfortable encounter with Mr. Chesterfield out of his mind. After all, as Abigail had correctly pointed out, it shouldn't matter if he had feelings for her since the only feelings that mattered in this case were hers. And after everything she'd told James, he knew with absolute certainty that he was the man she desired. And if her words didn't prove it, the two additional kisses they'd managed to share in secret this past week did.

Fervent and eager, Abigail left no doubt in his mind that their union would be a passionate one. And nothing thrilled him more. Which was probably why he arrived at the church on Saturday morning half an hour before the service was set to take place.

Having chosen to spend the last night of his bachelorhood at the house he'd be sharing from this day forward with his wife, he'd risen especially early on account of the restless excitement bubbling inside him. The clock on his dresser had shown only ten after five, so he'd tried to go back to sleep, only to fail. Deciding to read for a bit, he'd picked up the book he'd recently been keeping on his bedside table. Abigail had recommended it, a fascinating account of Captain Cook's travels to New Zealand.

"Never in a million years would I have supposed that this is the sort of literature you enjoy," he'd teasingly told her.

"Why? Because I'm a woman?"

"Of course not," he'd said while considering the leather bound tome with interest. "It's because so much of it takes place aboard a ship." When she'd looked puzzled, he'd said, "If I'm not mistaken, you told me just last week that you don't like sailing."

Her laughter had brightened her eyes and squeezed at his heart. "Reading about it is not exactly the same."

"Hmm. Miss Austen's novels take place on land though. Would you not prefer them instead?"

She'd placed both hands on her hips and regarded him suspiciously. "If I didn't know any better, I'd say that this is your way of trying to figure out why I prefer informative narratives rather than romantic nonsense."

He'd smirked. "My sisters seem to enjoy what you claim to be romantic nonsense. And if you must know, I've actually read a couple of Miss Austen's books myself." When Abigail's eyes had widened with disbelief, he'd leaned toward her and told her smugly, "I even happened to enjoy them."

Her gasp of surprise had made him grin. "I'll tell you what. If you read *Emma*, then I'll read this. Once we're done we'll exchange opinions."

She'd agreed, much to his delight, and they'd decided to allow two weeks for them both to finish their respective books.

It was seven by the time James decided to rise. He called for his valet, who brought him a much appreciated cup of hot coffee to start the day on, and then helped him dress. By eight o'clock, James was downstairs having breakfast and reading the morning paper. He was just about to get up from the table after finishing off a second slice of toast when the butler brought him a letter.

Recognizing the writing as Abigail's, he felt a rush of unease dart through him, but this was soon banished the moment he read her message.

My dearest James,

I thought I should let you know that the funeral is off, just in case you need to cancel any caskets you may have ordered without my knowing. Instead, I look forward to many long years of happiness by your side.

Yours always,

Abby

James smiled and tucked the missive into his jacket pocket. Most people would find such a letter morbid. The fact that Abigail didn't and that she actually encouraged this strange form of humor made her all the more interesting. She was fun and she was different and heaven help him if he wasn't falling for her in ways he never would have expected.

It was eleven o'clock by the time all the guests were seated in the pews at the church. Standing near the altar with William by his side, James waited expectantly for his bride to arrive. The doors at the far end of the aisle would open at any moment, they'd say their vows, endure a tedious wedding breakfast at Foxborough House, and finally embark on their happily ever after.

Someone coughed, the sound reverberating through the building. Fabric rustled as some of the guests shifted in their seats. William sighed but refrained from uttering a word. James caught Charles's gaze and started to panic. Surely she ought to have been here by now.

Retrieving his pocket watch, he took quick note of the time. It was ten after eleven. He glanced at the vicar, who raised his brows and shrugged his shoulders, which wasn't the least bit helpful.

And then the doors at the end of the aisle did start to open and James breathed a sigh of relief. Until he saw that Abigail was absent. Only her father, Lord Foxborough, appeared, and he was now walking swiftly toward him.

A strange and uncomfortable feeling grabbed hold of James's gut. He knew before Foxborough spoke that something dreadful had happened, for the look in the marquess's eyes revealed both anger and fear.

"What is it?" James asked. "Where's Abby?"

"She's been kidnapped," Foxborough whispered, so low only James and William would hear. "Mr. Chesterfield snatched her straight out of the carriage and whisked her away. They're on their way to Gretna Green as we speak."

A chill swept across James's shoulders as angst panic into his bones. And then, determined to reject the feeling, anger set it. He balled both hands into fists. "Thank you for letting me know."

He crossed to where his family sat, waiting for him to explain what was happening while murmurs began filling the air. "I'm heading to Scotland," he said, directing the comment mostly at Charles and his father.

"Good heavens," his mother exclaimed. "You can't do that. You're about to be married and—"

"Only if I can manage to find Abby."

His mother gasped and started saying something about causing a scandal, which was understandable since it apparently seemed impossible for any of her sons to marry without one. And while James sympathized, he hadn't the time to ease her concerns. He turned and headed toward the exit, almost reaching it when he realized he was being followed by Abigail's brother.

"We can take my carriage," Lance said as they burst out into the street. "It's right over there."

"I don't need your help," James told him icily.

"I'm offering it anyway," Lance said. "My phaeton will be faster than any of the cumbersome landaus."

Accepting the truth in his comment, James relented and followed Lance across the street to where the sportiest vehicle he'd ever seen stood waiting. It wasn't the most comfortable thing he'd ever sat in, he decided as Lance whipped the horses into motion. In fact, the speed at which it travelled combined with its spindly wheels made it a rather terrifying mode of transportation.

"You know," James said as they headed toward the north road, "Abby would be my wife by now if it weren't for your idiot friend." Perhaps talking would distract him from his visions of death and disaster at the hands of Lance's insane driving skills.

"Hence my eagerness to help you find her," Lance remarked. "Toby isn't so bad but he's not the right match for my sister. No matter how much he'd like to be."

James gritted his teeth. He wasn't particularly keen on resorting to murder, but he wasn't sure he'd be able to stop himself where Mr. Chesterfield was concerned. The foolish man had crossed a line and somehow, he was going to have to pay.

Chapter Six

ONE HOUR EARLIER (MORE or less) outside Foxborough House

"What the hell do you think you're doing?" Abigail asked as Tobias yanked her out of the carriage that was meant to convey her and her father to the church. "This is not the time for—"

"Mr. Chesterfield," her father called. "Release my daughter this instant!" The coachman clambered down from his box, ready to offer assistance while a pair of footmen hurried down the front steps of Foxborough House.

Tobias must have realized he was about to be stopped from whatever foolishness he was planning for he practically threw Abigail onto his horse as if she were a bale of hay being tossed onto a cart.

She landed belly down with a loud, "Oomph!"

Then Tobias mounted the steed himself. "I'm better for her than Mr. Townsbridge," he shouted, "so I'm taking her to Scotland in order to make her mine!" The horse reared back and Abigail screamed, convinced she would fall to her death. But the beast slammed its front hooves onto the ground and took off as if the devil himself were in pursuit.

A hand gripped her bottom, adjusting her position.

"Good God, Toby! Let me down!"

He ignored her completely. It didn't matter how much she kicked or screamed, he just kept riding. "I am going to kill you," she tried. "But before I do, I shall have you tarred and feathered." The horse didn't stop. In fact, it felt as though it ran faster as they left London behind and started along the north road. "I'll never forgive you for this, Toby. Do you hear me? I want to marry James!"

"No, you don't," Tobias finally muttered. "You're miserable when you're around him. But with me, you'll be happy."

"No, I won't!" She tried to grab at him with her hands in an effort to make him stop, but as she did so, she made a maneuver that caused her weight to distribute in such a way that she found herself falling.

"Dear God," Tobias shouted while she screamed in terror. And then she hit the ground with a thwack and the world she knew turned to darkness.

WHEN ABIGAIL CAME TO, she noticed three things. One, everything hurt; two, she was tucked into a comfortable bed; and three, the man who'd put her there stood too far away for her to hit.

"I'd like to strangle you right now," she said.

He spun away from the window he'd been looking out of and rushed to her side. "You're awake," he gasped with heartfelt concern. Taking a seat on the edge of the bed, he grabbed her hand and squeezed it tight. "I've been so dreadfully worried about you."

Abigail shook her head while trying to come to grips with what he had done. Avoiding another scandal would be impossible since she'd failed to appear at the church. People would talk and draw all sorts of conclusions. In truth, there was no way out of this mess that did not involve her being dragged through the mud in some way or other, most likely with James and the rest of her family in tow.

She glanced around the sparsely furnished room which contained just the bed, a chair, a small table, and a wash stand. "Where are we?"

A horse was neighing outside. "At the nearest inn I could find after you took your fall, perhaps fifteen miles from the city."

Bringing her palm to her forehead, Abigail took a moment to work out how long it would take for James to reach them. But doing so proved a challenge when she didn't even know how long it had been since they'd left Foxborough House.

Lowering her hand, she saw that her knuckles were grazed. At least Toby hadn't undressed her while she'd been unconscious. Beneath the blanket covering her, she still wore her wedding gown.

"You have to take me back right now," she said. The quicker she returned, the better. Or at least this was what she chose to believe.

Tobias just smiled. "Don't be silly, Abby. We both know your marrying Mr. Townsbridge would have been a dreadful mistake, and since you felt you had no choice in the matter, I realized there was nothing for it but to risk all in order to save you."

Abigail swallowed. His eyes were filled with adoration, his smile conveying both warmth and happiness. And she knew in that moment that Tobias didn't think he'd done anything wrong. Quite the opposite, actually. And this made her wary, because it made her wonder if perhaps James had been right about Tobias's feelings for her all along.

"But you didn't save me, Toby." She sat up and gave him the most forthright gaze she could manage. "I *wanted* to marry Mr. Townsbridge today."

"Of course you did," he murmured with something akin to compassion filling his eyes. "Your family's reputation was at stake. You had no choice but to do your best in order to minimize the scandal. Especially for Petra's sake. But everything will be better now."

Abigail sucked in a breath. "How does whisking me away make anything better?" she asked as she yanked her hand free from his grasp. Her eyes were starting to prick with the deep understanding that what he had done would ruin her every chance of salvaging an already fragile situation. Whatever prospects her sister might have had for a successful Season when she debuted were growing slimmer by the second.

"I'll make you happy," Tobias vowed. "I'll—"

"James would have made me happy," Abigail argued.

Tobias frowned and then he suddenly laughed. Not a humorous laugh but rather the kind that made Abigail want to shrink away into nothing. "I know you've just taken a hit to the head, Abby, but let's be honest. That man—" he practically spat those two words "—made you miserable. Hell, I've never seen you more unhappy than when you were in his company and *he* did that. He took away your sparkle, the *joie de vivre* that made you so dazzling. And I will never forgive him for that."

The anger in his voice seemed to come from somewhere deep inside. Abby stared. She'd never seen Tobias like this. He had always been charming and composed, but now...now he was like a thundercloud ready to send bolts of lightning in every direction.

"Toby," she told him gently, hoping to calm him. "I know you were acting in what you thought was my best interest today, but you have to take me home. I want to go back to London. I want to marry James."

"No." He made a decisive sweeping motion with his hand.

Abigail gaped at him, at this person she'd known for most of her life and who'd now transformed into someone she didn't recognize. "No?"

"After he compromised you at the Pratchard ball, you were horrified by the prospect of having to marry him. Then, when he came to call on you at your house and found me there, he was rude and condescending toward you, and when I happened upon the two of you in the park, it was clear that he was oppressing you and that you wished to be anywhere else but in his company. So forgive me for doing what most would consider completely unthinkable, but the very idea of Mr. James Townsbridge owning you makes me want to do bloody murder!"

Having risen during this tirade, Tobias raked a trembling hand through his hair and turned away. His back was rigid, his breathing ragged. Abigail watched him with mixed feelings as she thought back on James's courtship and how it must have looked from Tobias's perspective. As she did so, the lopsided world she'd awoken to seemed to right itself, for she finally understood his anger.

"It's true that James and I got off to a pretty bad start," Abigail said. She waited until she was sure Tobias was listening before she continued. "We didn't like each other much when we first met, I'll admit. Getting caught together in a compromising position was destined to make things worse. But the real problem was that we didn't really understand each other well, and I, at least, was too afraid to be honest. We've since moved past that, though. We've talked and gotten to know each other." She drew a deep breath. "When you met us in the park, I had a terrible headache. That is the only reason why I may have seemed unwell to you."

Unsure of what else to say, she stopped talking. A pause followed and then Tobias turned toward her. His expression was grim, but the anger from earlier seemed to have vanished. "Are you saying that I have misinterpreted the situation?"

Abigail nodded. "Yes. I believe you have." She watched his expression transform into one of dismay and then added, "There's no doubt in my mind that you meant well, Toby, but in truth, you have just made everything so much worse."

"I'm sorry." Tobias's gaze darted toward the window before returning to her. "I was only trying to help. I..." He closed his eyes on a sigh and dropped down onto the bed near her feet, causing her to bounce a little in response to his added weight. Leaning forward, he braced his forearms on his thighs and stared at the floor. "I want to make you happy and...I just wish..."

When he said nothing further, she pushed aside the blanket and swung her legs over the side of the bed so she could sit beside him. "When you offered for my hand last year, I believed you did it because you've never been close to your own family and marrying me would have made you part of mine. But there's more to it than that. Isn't there?"

It felt like an hour went by before he finally said, "I love you, Abby." His voice was pained and although he'd done something terribly wrong, she felt her heart break a little on his behalf. "The thought of you with another man kills me. And all because of my worthless brother. Had it not been for him your father would have accepted my suit, and you would now be my wife."

She flinched in response to his voice, now suddenly raised and awfully loud in the small space they were in. The fury that burned inside him was shocking, as was the thought of how different things might have been if his brother had not tarnished the Chesterfield name.

A shudder went through her, for she knew she would have married Tobias had her father allowed it, and lost her chance with James.

"You've always been a wonderful friend, Toby." When he raised his head and glared at her with accusing eyes wrought with heartache, she hastened to add, "I love you dearly, though not in the way you wish but more like a brother."

With a grunt, he stood and went to the window. "A lot of good that does me."

She understood his misery. When she hadn't believed James would ever return her affection, she'd been dreadfully unhappy as well. Unrequited love was no simple thing. It could plague the mind and the soul and lead to discontentment of the worst possible kind.

"I'm sorry," she said, unsure of how to help him. "You're a wonderful man: kind, considerate and—"

"Stop." He didn't look at her, but she could tell by his tone she'd said the wrong thing. "None of that matters."

"Of course it does," she tried, hating the uncomfortable atmosphere clinging to the walls and the awkwardness wedged between them. "One day, you'll find a woman who will fall in love with those qualities. A woman who will love you as you deserve to be loved."

"Why the hell should I care about that when she won't be you?" he shouted with such brutal force and suddenness that Abigail scrambled back onto the bed.

Staring at him, at his flattened mouth, clenched jaw, and flashing eyes, she felt a tremor of fear slide down her back. "I...I..." She shook her head and frantically searched for the right thing to say.

He moved toward her and she scooted back, until she was pressed up against the headboard. "Why don't you love me as you should, Abby?" His sneer was low and full of menace.

Abigail's heart pounded against her ribs. This wasn't the man she knew. This wasn't the amicable friend with whom she'd laughed on countless occasions or on whose shoulder she'd cried at the age of twelve when her dog had died. This person who stood before her, now leaning in, was someone else entirely – a stranger she did not recognize.

"As you say," he continued. "I'm kind and considerate. Wonderful even, by your account." His knee landed on the mattress and then he placed both hands on either side of her, caging her in as he stared down into her eyes. "But I'm still not good enough for you."

"Toby," she said, her voice weaker than she would have liked. "Let's talk about this. Let's—"

"Do you know what I think, Abby?" His gaze dropped to the edge of her neckline and for a second, Abigail forgot how to breathe. When he looked up, he wore the most unsettling expression she'd ever seen. It was smug and full of determination. "I think you could learn to love me."

She barely managed to comprehend his meaning before his mouth was on hers, hard and unyielding. Dismayed and suddenly terrified, Abby grabbed at his shoulders and tried to push him away. But he was heavier than she and relentless in his assault.

Straddling her hips, he held her down with his weight. A whimper escaped her and she clutched at his face in a blind attempt to twist him away. But her battered body was weak from the fall, and as pain arched through her, he grabbed her wrists and forced them down onto the mattress.

With no resources left, she did the only thing she could think of and bit his lip.

He released her instantly, and for a second, she believed she'd won. But then she saw the look in his eyes – dark, pained, and full of anger. "That was a foolish mistake," he murmured.

Abigail's blood ran cold. Trembling, she tried to gauge the space between Tobias and the door. Was there any way for her to escape him without his catching her first? It was unlikely. But she had to try. So she launched herself forward only to feel his hand curl possessively around her ankle. Before she managed to leave the bed, she was yanked back. A scream broke from her throat as she landed face down, kicking and flailing.

"Hold still and be quiet, damn you!"

"Never!" She screamed again, praying that someone would hear and come to her rescue.

"So be it then," he gritted. Climbing onto her, he held her down and pressed her face into the bedclothes. She kept trying to reach behind her back, grabbing at what she supposed must be his thigh, but nothing she did made him budge. And then he was tying something around her mouth – a length of fabric. His cravat, perhaps?

Abigail tried to scream once again but this time, only a muffled sound emerged. Eyes wet with tears, she bucked and twisted, hoping to somehow dislodge him so she could escape. But then she felt him shift, rising a little and...

Oh God!

A choked sob escaped her as Tobias shoved up her skirts. "This is the only way," he said. "Once I've claimed you, you'll have no choice in the matter. Nobody will."

Despite the raw ache gripping her arms and shoulders, Abby reached behind herself once again and tried to hit him. Dear heaven above, he was going to force her to get what he wanted. "No!" Her shout was barely audible against the fabric muffling her voice.

"You have the most gorgeous bottom I've ever seen," he said, settling one palm against it and letting his fingers sink into the flesh. He shifted again, muttered a curse, and was suddenly yanking at one of her stockings. "I told you to stay still but you just won't listen." Grabbing her wrists he pulled them together in front of her head and wound the stocking around them until they were tied together.

"Please," she tried, almost choking with helpless despair.

"Shh..." The anger was suddenly gone from his voice, replaced by a husky whisper. He leaned over her. His lips brushed her cheek. "I wish I could make this good for you, Abby, but I just don't have the time. So please forgive me."

She tried once again to move, but weakness overwhelmed her. A bone-shattering angst, the likes of which she'd never known, dug its claws into her soul.

She closed her eyes and thought of James.

And then the door to the room crashed open.

"GET YOUR BLOODY HANDS off of her, you bastard!"

Having followed a trail that consisted of two eye-witness accounts and a white silk slipper he'd found on the side of the road, James had leapt from Lance's phaeton the moment they'd pulled up to the first inn. Only to learn, after a great deal of hollering, that Abigail and Chesterfield weren't there.

So he'd hired a horse in the hope of quickening his pace and left Lance to catch up as best as he could. James's heart had pounded faster than the hooves thundering against the ground while all sorts of awful imaginings filled his head. But nothing was as bad as what he eventually found when he entered the second inn and was told that a man and woman matching Chesterfield's and Abigail's descriptions had indeed rented a room.

"You mustn't disturb them," the innkeeper had shouted above the noise of the men who were eating and drinking in the taproom.

James had simply headed for the stairs and proceeded to climb them two at a time.

"They're newlyweds and according to the husband, his poor wife took a dangerous tumble while—"

James didn't hear anything else. The rage pouring through him and the fear he harbored on Abigail's behalf made it impossible for him to focus on anything else. His muscles flexed and strained beneath his skin, and his hands fairly trembled with the need to do violence.

"Which door?" he somehow managed to ask.

The innkeeper, who'd followed him and now wisely realized he'd better speak up or risk having James barge in on someone who didn't deserve it, pointed toward a door at the end of the hallway.

James stalked toward it, hands clenched and jaw set. Without breaking his stride, he raised his foot and brought it down next to the handle, producing a massive bang as the door broke away from the frame.

With one quick scan, James took in the scene before him: Abigail, trussed like a lamb about to be slaughtered, her rumpled gown pushed up around her waist to reveal her bare buttocks, Chesterfield kneeling between her thighs, one hand on her back while the other worked the buttons on his breeches.

With a roar that seemed to come from some primitive place deep inside him, James leapt for Chesterfield's throat. "Get your bloody hands off of her, you bastard!"

Chesterfield's eyes went wide. He froze for a second, then raised his hands to defend himself. But kneeling as he was on the bed, his balance was poor, so the moment James struck him, he tumbled backward onto the floor, gasping and sputtering while clasping his neck.

"You like hurting women, do you, you lecherous bugger?" James fell to his knees next to Chesterfield, pulled back his fist then slammed it forward with all the might he possessed. It struck its target with a loud crack. A howl splintered the air but James ignored it. Now that he was hitting this man who'd been seconds away from violating Abigail, he could not seem to stop. There was a hunger inside him that needed satisfaction, a thirst for blood that had to be quenched, and a fog in his brain that made him oblivious to anything else.

It wasn't until someone pulled him back and away from his target that James was able to see the mangled state of Chesterfield's face. His eyes were swollen shut, his nose turned slightly sideways, his lip and cheek torn open, and...he didn't look conscious. Blood was everywhere, on Chesterfield's face and on James's knuckles.

Shaking, James stared at Lance who was muttering something important about his sister. A flash of bright light exploded behind James's eyes, narrowing everything down to one point. He turned away, searching for Abigail. She was sitting up now, staring at him in stricken silence. Her skirts had been pulled down, thank God, her gag and restraints removed, no doubt by her brother. Tears streaked her cheeks as she rocked back and forth while hugging herself.

"I'm sorry," James croaked. "I...I..." His throat closed, preventing him from saying anything further.

A solid hand grasped his shoulder. "You did the right thing," Lance said, his voice tight with restraint. "And if you hadn't, I would have."

James nodded and stepped toward Abigail, unsure if his feet would carry his weight but knowing he had to be near her.

"I'm sorry," he said again as he sank to his knees before her. And he was sorry. Not for hurting Chesterfield, but for what she'd had to go through and for not being able to help her sooner.

Clasping her hands, he gazed into her watery eyes and felt his heart shatter. Her lips were trembling, her right cheek grazed so badly it glistened with un-spilled blood.

A lump the size of an orange lodged itself in his throat, and his own eyes stung with tears. "He won't hurt you again." Bringing Abigail's hands to his lips, he kissed her knuckles, her fingers, her palms. "No one will ever hurt you again, my darling." His voice cracked with emotion. "I swear it."

Her only response was a ragged breath.

"I, um," Lance murmured. Standing near Chesterfield, who was still passed out on the floor, he shifted as if uncertain of how to approach the subject he wished to address. He cleared his throat. "I realize this is a difficult moment, but there are some practical matters that must be handled without delay."

James knew he was right. So although he was far from ready to deal with the ramifications of what had occurred, he stood and faced Abigail's brother. "I ought to call him out." He jutted his chin in Chesterfield's direction. "But I'd rather have him arrested, I think."

Lance nodded. "I'll see to it that someone fetches the local magistrate." He glanced at his sister, his expression going thoughtful before he added, "You have to marry right away and yet...I fear her return to London will be disastrous. People will want to know what happened and will either figure it out or draw their own conclusions. Either way, it doesn't look good in terms of salvaging her reputation."

"I can take her to Arlington House. It's not far from here and the servants there are loyal. If you can—"

"Townsbridge." Lance stared at him as if he'd gone mad. "You cannot think of doing something like that before she's your wife. It's...it's...I mean..."

"Would you rather we head back to the church?"

"No. Of course not. But we could take her to Foxborough House and have the two of you marry there."

"I don't want to be gawked at or pitied or questioned," Abby muttered. "I just want privacy."

It was the first thing she'd said since James had arrived, and the sound of her voice, so lifeless and faint, caused his anger to rise again. "We're going to Arlington," he told Lance decisively. "Inform our families, if you will."

Lance didn't look remotely happy but James didn't care.

"I'll also have to try and acquire a special license on your behalf," Lance said. "The one you were meant to use today won't work in another parish."

Damnation. James hadn't thought about that but Lance was right. "Fine." Reaching into his jacket pocket he retrieved thirty pounds and handed the money to Lance. "This should help butter up the archbishop. You'll need my father's help, of course, in order to sign for it."

Lance pocketed the coins and crossed to Abigail. "If all goes well, you and James will be married tomorrow." He bent and kissed her cheek, then turned to James. "I'll give the innkeeper a quick account of what happened on my way out and ask him to call the magistrate."

"Thank you, Lance." Seeing the hesitance in the younger man's gaze as he gave Abigail one final glance, James said, "I'll protect her with my life."

They shared a quick look then Lance was off.

A groan came from where Chesterfield lay, causing Abigail to flinch. "Can you stand?" James asked her.

She nodded and pushed herself slowly away from the bed. When she swayed, James quickly reached out to steady her by her elbow. "Here," he murmured, handing her his handkerchief so she could blow her nose. Chesterfield emitted another groan and James realized he was now moving his legs. It wouldn't be long before he was fully awake.

As if sensing the same thing, Abigail clutched hold of James's hand. "I don't want to face him. I just want to leave." Her breaths grew louder and faster. "Can we please go? Can we—"

"Yes. Of course." James scooped her up in his arms and marched into the hallway. A couple of brawny fellows were approaching from the stairs.

"You Mr. Townsbridge?" one of them asked. When James answered in the affirmative, the man said, "The innkeeper sent us up to keep an eye on the troublemaker."

Thanking the men, James descended the stairs where the innkeeper himself was ready to assist. "I'm sorry about earlier," he said. "I didn't realize the man you were chasing had kidnapped your wife. The gall of him to snatch her like that right after the wedding! I'm just surprised you didn't kill him."

"I was tempted," James said once he'd set Abigail on her feet. He didn't correct the man with regard to their marital status since Lance had obviously lied in order to protect his sister's reputation for as long as possible. "If you could please write to me at this address and inform me of Mr. Chesterfield's arrest," he said as he handed the innkeeper his card, "I'd appreciate it."

"Of course." The innkeeper slipped the card into a book he kept on a tall writing desk near the front door. "I believe your friend left his phaeton for you to use and took a horse instead."

Relieved to hear it, James thanked the man and escorted Abigail out of the inn to where Lance's sporty vehicle stood waiting.

Chapter Seven

IT DIDN'T TAKE LONG for them to reach Arlington House. An hour, perhaps, by Abigail's estimation. James didn't say much during the journey, which was still considerably more than what she'd managed to say. His focus seemed to be on the horses, though she did feel the weight of his gaze from time to time as she looked out over the wide open fields.

Her tears had dried and her body gone completely numb.

Watching birds soar through the sky while the sun warmed her face, she wondered if life would somehow go on without her, for the truth of the matter was, she knew she had died inside today. It didn't matter how caring James seemed or how understanding. She'd trusted Tobias and he'd betrayed her in the worst possible way. He'd stolen the anticipation she'd had for her wedding night. The very idea of being bedded now, by any man, caused bile to rise in her throat. And she wasn't sure how she would ever be able to tell James that.

"Maybe we shouldn't marry," she said that evening when he came to check on her. The housekeeper, a lovely middle-aged woman named Mrs. Anderson, had shown Abigail to a pretty room furnished in pale blue colors. A maid had brought some delicious stew which Abigail had eaten while waiting for a hot bath to be drawn. Later, once she'd finished bathing, Mrs.

Anderson had given her a nightgown and a robe belonging to one of the maids.

James frowned in response to Abigail's comment and moved toward her. When she stepped away, deliberately trying to avoid his embrace, he stilled. "Why?"

There were too many answers to that question. *Because I'm tarnished. Because I'm afraid I will always see* him *when you touch me. Because you deserve so much better than me. Because...*

She thought she'd gotten past being nervous when she was with James, but now, with his gaze intensely fixed upon her, her belly turned over and it was suddenly hard to breathe. Hoping to block him out, she gave him her back.

"Abby?" His voice was soft and gentle. Careful, even.

Getting the necessary words out was nearly impossible, so she was grateful when he didn't push her to answer more quickly than she was able. Instead, he just waited, until she finally managed to say, "I don't ever want you to hate me."

There was a pause. A long one. And then he said. "I suppose it's only natural for you to worry that I might do so after what happened. But the truth is, nothing in the world would be more impossible for me than to hate you, Abby. Not when I care for you as much as I do."

He'd never told her he loved her. Then again, she'd never told him either. But in that moment, she rather wished he had. Although, to be fair, she wanted him to be honest as well. And now she would have to be honest too.

"Everything's different now, James." She spoke to the wall, but she knew he listened intently from somewhere behind her. "I don't think I can..." Unable to say it, she waved one hand, as if the gesture would fill in the blanks.

"Shh... It's all right. Just let me be your friend for now. That's all."

"But won't you want to..." She waved her hand again.

"Not if you don't."

Air rushed from her lungs on a sigh of relief. "Thank you."

"Just get some rest for now and call me if you need anything." She sensed him hesitate as if deciding whether or not he ought to say something more or possibly offer some show of affection. But then she heard him cross to the door between their two bedrooms. "I'm prepared to give you as much time as you need to recover from this. Our wedding night can wait until you are ready."

"What if that day never comes?" she asked. But she spoke too late and her words were too soft for him to hear.

THE FOLLOWING DAY WENT by in such a blur that Abigail hardly had time to think of her horrid encounter with Tobias. James's parents and siblings arrived around noon, and half an hour later one of the Foxborough carriages rolled up the drive, bringing her parents, Petra, and Lance to Arlington House.

A young vicar who looked like he'd barely gotten out of seminary school conducted the service. James mentioned at one point that he was newly appointed, which probably explained why it took him so long to ensure the special license was up to snuff. Abby barely recalled agreeing to be James's wife, but she supposed she must have at some point, because everyone was suddenly wishing her well.

She tried to smile and look normal. It was almost as if she were standing outside her own body, watching a tableau play out before her. Thankfully, nobody mentioned the previous day's occurrence. She'd been especially worried her mother or sister might pull her aside at some point to inquire about her wellbeing. But they didn't. And then it was suddenly time for them to take their leave.

Abigail stood on the steps of her new home with James by her side and waved goodbye. She felt nothing as she did so. No happiness or sadness. Just an empty void.

"Nobody asked me to tell them what happened," she whispered as the carriages rolled down the drive.

"I told them not to."

She was grateful for that, for it had made this day so much easier to bear.

"Shall we have some tea together in the library?" James asked as they headed back inside.

All Abigail wanted to do was retreat to her bedchamber, crawl into bed, and forget the world existed. But he deserved better than that. Especially on his wedding day. So she nodded and let him escort her.

"I've always loved this room," he told her a short while later once the maid who'd brought their tea had departed. Surveying the books in the bookcases lining the walls, James paused occasionally to read the spines while Abigail watched from her spot on a red velvet sofa. He glanced over his shoulder and smiled with a boyish gleam in his eyes. "When I was younger, my siblings and I would play a game of sorts. I can show you, if you like."

It was quite possibly the very last thing she felt like doing at the moment, but once again, she reminded herself that the least she could do for James was make an effort at being somewhat agreeable. "All right," she said, wishing she'd managed to answer with a bit more enthusiasm.

But if he noticed her dull tone, he chose not to show it. Instead he grinned, the exuberance in every line of his face causing warmth to seep through her veins. Or maybe that was just the tea starting to have an effect?

"Here's what we do," he told her brightly while pulling a series of books off the shelves. "We're going to mix these up and then take turns finding the words we need." Piling the books in his arms, he carried them to the table in front of the sofa, then went to a cabinet where he located some paper and a couple of pencils. "You'll need these as well." He handed her one of the pencils along with a piece of paper.

Increasingly intrigued, Abigail straightened her spine and waited for him to sit. He glanced at the vacant spot beside her, but rather than claim it, he lowered himself to an adjacent chair. A twinge of disappointment raced through her. On one hand she wanted him close, but on the other, she didn't. It was most disconcerting and horribly confusing.

"Now then," he said, distracting her from her thoughts and emotions. "You have to pick a book at random, flip it open, select the first word from the first paragraph that draws your eye, and write it down. You then pick another book and pick the second word from the first paragraph that draws your eye. And so on."

"Sounds simple enough," she said.

"It is. Shall I go first?"

"By all means." She reached for her teacup and drank while James selected his first book. Placed face down on the table and with their spines turned sideways, she was unable to read their titles.

"Your turn," he said about five minutes later. A lopsided grin pulled at his lips and for half a second, Abigail forgot her ordeal with Tobias and how much she now dreaded being intimate with her husband. All she knew was that her heart was swelling, tripling in size and filling with warmth.

But then the clock on the fireplace mantle chimed, breaking the spell.

She shook her head and reached for a book. Plato's *The Republic*, she realized. Flipping it open at random, she picked her first word and wrote it down.

"What do you have?" James asked once she'd finished leafing through *A Midsummer Night's Dream, Henry IV, Pride and Prejudice, Northanger Abbey, The Iliad,* and *Domestic Medicine.*

"Nothing that makes any sense."

"You're allowed to rearrange the words in any order."

Pursing her lips, Abigail studied the seven words she'd jotted down. She tilted her head in thought and then suddenly smiled when she noticed a possible sentence. Clearing her throat, she read, "Caesar must go equipped with violent words."

James laughed. "That's brilliant." Eyes gleaming with mischief, he gave his attention to his own piece of paper. "Here's mine." He met her gaze fleetingly and then read, "These brokenhearted people have beheaded your furniture."

Abigail felt the edge of her mouth start to twitch and then a wave of energy rose up her throat, demanding release, and before she knew it she was laughing so hard her belly began to ache. "Goodness, that's good," she gasped as she fell back against the sofa and gave her eyes a quick wipe.

"Shall we have another go?" James asked. He was watching her with keen amusement and...something she couldn't quite place though it did something rather lovely to her insides.

"Absolutely," she said with a smile. "But this time I get to go first."

IT WAS PAST MIDNIGHT by the time James escorted Abigail upstairs. They'd taken dinner in the library while using the books to create additional sentences, like *hysterical old gentlemen love to do justice*. As he'd hoped, the exercise had allowed Abigail to forget the memories that plagued her so she could relax and have fun. For a few wonderful hours, she'd returned to being the vibrant woman he'd come to adore, and this gave him hope.

Reaching her bedchamber door, he stepped back and offered a bow. She needed time, perhaps more than he wanted to accept at the moment. But he knew patience would be the only way forward if they were to stand a chance of happiness together. Her mind and soul had taken a terrible blow. He'd known that the moment he looked into her eyes yesterday at the inn and saw nothing but hopeless despair. But he wasn't going to give up on her or on them. He'd do whatever he had to in order to help her conquer the fear that now gripped her.

"Sleep well, Abby." He would not enter her room or do anything else to upset the joy they'd found in each other's company this evening. "I look forward to breakfasting with you in the morning."

"As do I," she told him. A sad smile touched her lips and for a brief moment he thought she might say something else. But then she turned away and the bedchamber door closed, leaving him alone in the hallway.

James blew out a breath and continued toward his own room. The mountain he had to climb was steep, and so far, he'd taken only a couple of steps. Tomorrow he'd take two more. Hopefully in the right direction.

But when he woke in the morning, he wasn't quite sure if she'd favor a ride to an old castle ruin or a picnic down by the lake, so he decided to ask instead of deciding for her.

"Could we not just stay here?" she asked while buttering her toast. When she'd arrived in the dining room ten minutes earlier, her hesitant expression had made him realize that whatever progress he thought he'd made last night had been miniscule. Telling her that he'd received word of Chesterfield's arrest didn't help, but James was determined to be open and honest with her, even though he knew she hated being reminded of what her former friend had done.

"We could, but I'd much rather take advantage of the good weather. Autumn will come before we know it, and then we'll be forced to remain indoors."

"I suppose that's true." Abigail took a bite of her toast. Her gaze, James noted, was aimed at the table instead of at him. "Could we not combine the two options then?"

Instinctively, he reached for her hand, then stopped himself and let his own fall. "Of course we can." He leaned back in his chair and watched as she drank some tea. "I'll ask Cook to prepare a basket for us and make sure the carriage is ready to leave by...shall we say eleven?"

"All right."

"All right," he echoed. Castle Islington was exactly the sort of place to stir one's imagination with endless possibilities of adventure, mystery, and romance. As children, he and his siblings had loved exploring what remained of the structure while their parents reclined on a blanket nearby, either napping or reading in the shade of an elm.

And because of this sentimental attachment he had to the place, he was glad to see the excitement in Abigail's eyes when he handed her down from the carriage later and she took her first look at what had once been, to him, a pirate ship, a Roman fortress, and a buried temple.

"This is splendid," she said as she walked toward it. Most of the walls still stood, some more intact than others, but the roof, floors, and doors – anything made of wood– had long since rotted away. Ivy and other creepers covered the stone in a blanket of green, and moss grew between the cracks in the shade. "Is it safe to climb those steps?"

"I think so," James said as he crossed to the stairs leading up to the battlements, "but let me go first." He didn't like that there was no railing – an odd thing since he'd not given the lack of safety measures any thought as a child.

"When was the last time you came here?" she asked.

"Ten years ago, I should think. Charles wasn't with us because he'd decided to spend that summer travelling the

Continent. So it was just William, Sarah, Athena, and me." He grinned as he recalled how disastrous that outing had been. "The weather looked fine when we set out, but then, out of nowhere, it started pouring. Everyone got soaked and..." He laughed. "As we hurried back to the carriage, Athena slipped on the grass, landed on her bottom, and skidded at least a yard." He stepped onto the battlement and offered Abigail his hand, which she thankfully took. "Of course, her dress was ruined, and since she's never liked being the odd one out, she quickly made sure we joined her."

Abigail stared at him wide-eyed. "How on earth did she manage that?"

"By throwing mud at us."

"What?"

He chuckled. "Sounds awful, I know, but it was all in good sport." Turning, he braced himself with his feet apart and allowed the view to impress him. Abigail's hand was still nestled firmly in his, so he hardly dared move for fear she'd pull away. "Now tell me honestly," he murmured with every intention of keeping her mind on him and this place. "What do you think?"

She was silent for a while before she finally said, "I think it's glorious." And then she turned to him with the brightest smile he'd ever seen, and it was all he could do not to lean in and kiss her.

But since he feared that would ruin the moment, he simply replied with, "I think so as well."

"I WAS WONDERING," ABIGAIL said later that afternoon when they returned to Arlington House, "if you'd like to play a game of chess with me." She'd enjoyed exploring the castle with James, then sitting on a blanket with him afterward while they ate their lunch. They'd talked about their family in greater detail than before, and she'd shared some of the pranks she and her siblings had played on each other. Now that they were home, she felt the magic of the day start to fade and the weight of reality take its place. But if James was willing to help her forget, then maybe she could ignore it for just a while longer.

"Sounds like a challenge," he said as he led the way into a cozy parlor. Crossing to the sideboard, he picked up a pair of glasses while she took a seat on a chair upholstered in pale green silk damask. "Drink?"

She wasn't used to imbibing except during meals, yet the prospect of doing so now with her husband was remarkably tempting. "Just a small one, please."

The cheeky smile with which he responded was thoroughly dashing. And she wished. Oh, how she wished, that Lance had never brought Tobias home from Eton with him all those years ago, that she'd never known him and he'd never had the chance to ruin her wedding, her life, her marriage.

"Abby?"

Blinking, she glanced up at James. He was holding one of the glasses toward her and frowning. "Forgive me. I must have been woolgathering." She took the glass and set it to her lips.

"I thought a sherry might suit you best," he said.

"It's very tasty," she agreed and took another sip. "Sweet and delicious."

Something in his eyes shifted and darkened until it turned positively molten. Her skin heated in response and her heart beat faster. Her need for him was as real as her reluctance to let him touch her. She hated being like this and tried to think of something to say, but then he turned away and strode to a cabinet. When he returned, the brief desire he'd shown had been thoroughly quashed and replaced by a welcoming smile.

"You mentioned chess," he said. Placing a wooden set on the table before her, he claimed the chair opposite hers. His smile transformed to a smirk and his eyes lit with a new kind of passion. "Perhaps I should have told you, I've yet to meet a player experienced enough to beat me."

"I dare you to try," Abigail replied dryly as she moved the pawn in front of her king one step forward. He took a moment to consider, then moved the pawn in front of his bishop. She immediately countered by putting her knight into motion.

"Is that a spider crawling over your backrest?" James asked half an hour later.

Abigail instinctively turned, saw nothing, and returned her attention to the chess board. Her eyes narrowed. "Did you move my bishop?"

"What?" He pressed one hand to his chest and gave her a pitiful look. "I'd never do something like that."

And yet she knew...she just knew the piece had not been where it was now before she'd turned away. "There never was a spider, was there?" Of course there hadn't been. The maids would never allow such a creature to survive inside the house. And since this was the case, she moved her knight two places forward and five to the left to claim James's rook.

"Hey!" He stared at her in disbelief. "You can't do that. It's one step forward and two to the left if you want to go in that direction, which puts your knight right here on this vacant square."

She gave him a smug little smile. "If you can cheat at this game, then so can I."

"Oh, really?" His lips twitched with a hint of the laughter to come. "Well, in that case, I'll just move my bishop over here and declare the game over. Checkmate!"

Abigail pulled a throw cushion into her lap and tossed it directly at his head. "I would have beaten you fair and square, you know."

"In your dreams," he replied, tossing the cushion right back.

Dodging it, Abigail turned in her seat. And came face to face with the biggest spider she'd ever seen. "Ahhh!" She leapt up off the sofa, banging her knee in the process and knocking over most of the chess pieces.

"Told you," James said with a laugh as he went to collect the arachnid. "I'll be right back."

"So, you didn't move my bishop?" she asked when he returned to the parlor.

He eyed her for a second, then rocked back on his heels and shrugged his shoulders. "Well..."

"You scoundrel!"

He just stood there grinning at her. And before she knew it she was grinning as well. "I want a re-match," she finally said when she managed to catch her breath.

"Very well. Perhaps after dinner?"

She agreed. And when they played again later that evening she won, though she rather suspected this was not a very fair game either. But whether or not it was, she didn't really mind because she'd had fun, though she vowed to one day catch her husband red-handed as he meddled with the pieces.

After packing the game away together, he escorted her up the stairs to her bedchamber door. There he bid her good night in much the same manner as the previous evening, allowing her to avoid her marital duties for the second day in a row.

And so it continued for several days, until it made more sense to count the weeks. She knew he was being incredibly generous. By law, he had every right to demand she let him into her bed. But he didn't. Instead, he gave her friendship, understanding and an overwhelming amount of patience. He walked with her, rode with her, told her of his childhood, and listened when she spoke of hers. And it occurred to her one day that the man, who'd been so incredibly handsome he'd once made her fear being sick in his company, had become something more than a person to whom she was strongly attracted. He'd become her entire world, and she loved him more fiercely than she'd ever loved anyone else.

Chapter Eight

THEY'D BEEN MARRIED for six weeks, James realized one evening while he and Abigail took turns making up silly sentences from a stack of books she'd picked out. Sipping his brandy, he watched her find a word in *Gulliver's Travels*, her nose twitching a little as she set her pencil to paper and jotted it down.

They'd formed a companionable bond. And while he believed it would help them be happy together, he never stopped hoping there could be more. Occasionally, he wondered if he ought to risk pulling her into his arms for a kiss. But then he'd worry that doing so might destroy what they had. And he truly loved what they had.

Hell. He loved her. And he would do anything – anything at all—to make sure she didn't feel threatened by anyone ever again. Certainly not by him. So he kept his distance and did his best to hide the desire he felt for her. But it wasn't easy when she was right there – his wife, for heaven's sake – his to have if that was what he wanted. And he did want, but he wanted her to want as well.

"Your turn," she said, her gorgeous blue eyes dazzling him with their brilliance.

He smiled and set his glass aside, then gave his attention to the task at hand. These moments they shared were special and he cherished each one. But tonight his heart felt oddly heavy, as if weighed down by defeat. And yet he still managed to laugh when she read her line, even though he rather felt like weeping.

If she sensed something wrong, she didn't address it. Instead, she chatted about all sorts of curious things when he led her upstairs to her bedchamber later, from the correct density of whipped cream to her favorite embroidery technique to the need she felt for a longer handle on her pall-mall mallet.

"I'm sure one can be fashioned," he said with a weary sigh when they reached her door. As usual, he stepped away so he wouldn't be tempted to press his advances, and prepared to retire to his own room. "We can discuss it in the morning, Abby. For now, I shall bid you good night."

"I...I rather thought..." Her voice quivered in the dimly lit hallway.

The caution with which she spoke, bordering on nervous anxiousness, pricked his awareness. His gaze sharpened and he looked at her – really looked at her for the first time since they'd left the library ten minutes earlier. And he saw that she looked as lost and uncertain as she had when they'd first been introduced.

Disconcerted, he reached for her hand and gave it a comforting squeeze. "Is something the matter?"

"No. No, I'm fine."

But she didn't really sound fine. In fact, she sounded as if she'd rather crawl under the carpet and hide. James frowned.

What on earth was going on? She'd been perfectly normal before in the library, yet now...

"What is it then?" he asked more gruffly than he'd intended.

She licked her lips and he muttered a silent curse. If she would only refrain from being so bloody tempting and—

"I was wondering if you might like to spend some more time with me tonight." She cleared her throat and dropped her gaze. "In my bedchamber, that is."

James stood like a statue, utterly still and afraid to move. Although her face was averted and the only available light came from an oil lamp he carried, he could see her face had turned a bright shade of red.

"Are you suggesting...that is...what I mean to say...or rather, what I need to know, is um..." Christ! He'd no idea speaking could be so difficult. Least of all when he wasn't sure how to obtain the information he needed without sounding crass or desperate.

She raised her chin just enough to meet his gaze with what had to be tremendous courage, considering the creased lines on her forehead, the way her teeth caught her lower lip, and the convulsive way she swallowed. To say she felt completely unmoored would probably be a tremendous understatement.

And yet in spite of this, she managed to say, "I know I've made life difficult for you, and I must have given you plenty of reason to second guess marrying me."

"No, Abby. I—"

"Please. Let me finish." She took a deep breath. "The weeks since our wedding have been the best weeks of my life. And you, James, have been wonderful. In truth, I doubt there's another man in the world who would have been as understanding as you have been. You accepted me as I was and did your best to help me through the sort of experience that's bound to leave scars.

"Before you and I were properly introduced, I always admired you from a distance. You were the handsomest man I'd ever seen. Just being in your presence reduced me to a blithering idiot." She gave a low chuckle and he took the opportunity to squeeze her hand. "But I've gotten over that for the most part, and now that I know you better, I think it's time to let you know my heart belongs to no one but you. I love you, James, with all that I am, and I'd like to be more than the woman who happens to sleep in the room next to yours. I want to—"

The restraint James had put on himself since their wedding finally snapped. Sweeping his arm around his wife's waist, he lowered his mouth to hers and kissed her with all the pent-up need he possessed. He crushed her lips with his own and pressed his body to hers until he was sure she knew how eager he was to love her. God, how he'd longed for this moment. Looking back, he wasn't quite sure how he'd managed to keep his distance from her for this long. Not that it mattered. The only thing he cared about right now was that she was kissing him back, her fingers raking through his hair while soft, throaty murmurs escaped her.

"Abby..." He whispered her name as he hugged her close, the oil lamp swinging from his hand and causing the light to flicker. "I love you more than words can say." His voice cracked with emotion and he placed a soft kiss on her cheek, forcing himself to think of her and not of his own desire. So he breathed her in, loving the scent of honey and chamomile in her hair, and asked the one question he knew could ruin what promised to be an incredible evening. "Are you sure you're ready?"

There was a pause, during which he was certain his heart stopped beating. And then she said, "Yes. I'm sure. I want this, James."

He was tempted to ravish her right then and there. Instead, he deliberately reined in his fervor and quietly led her into her bedchamber. There he set the oil lamp on top of a dresser and finally closed the door. How he approached this first time between them would likely determine how willing she'd be to let him bed her in the future. So he knew he had to be gentle. And he also knew he had to keep her mind focused on him and the pleasure he meant to give her.

With this in mind, he started by pushing a stray strand of hair away from her brow. His hand scraped her skin in the process, moved over her ear, and settled more fully against her cheek. "I love you," he told her, then he kissed her again, this time with the sort of languor that suggested he had all the time in the world to explore her mouth with his own. And when he felt that the time was right, when she seemed relaxed and pliant in his arms, he kissed his way down the side of her neck and began unfastening her dress.

ABIGAIL HADN'T KNOWN where this evening would lead when she and James left the library earlier, but somehow, before she'd reached the foot of the stairs, she'd realized the time had come for them to be husband and wife in truth.

During the past six weeks, she'd forged a closer bond with him than she'd ever shared with anyone else. Day by day, her attachment to him had grown, as had her longing to connect with him on a deeper level.

And so she'd made her decision, and proceeded to speak of nonsensical things in an effort to focus on something besides her nerves. She couldn't help the jitters tumbling through her even though she knew being shy and worried was silly. James knew her better than anyone and there was no doubt in her mind that he would be a considerate lover or that she'd enjoy the experience.

So it really shouldn't have surprised her when every concern she'd had about how to address the subject of their lovemaking had been swept aside the moment he'd kissed her out in the hallway. It almost made her wish she'd told him she was open to his advances sooner.

His lips left hers and she uttered an unhappy whimper.

"Don't worry," he told her with a wry smile, "I'm just untying my cravat."

She watched in mesmerized silence as he unwound the long length of fabric and tossed it aside. He met her gaze head on as he reached up to push her gown down over her shoulders.

The garment fell to the floor with a whoosh that caused a surprised gasp to spring from her throat. James's eyes smoldered with deep appreciation, and the edge of his mouth curved into a roguish smile. Abigail's heart fluttered wildly against her breast.

"Seems to me I'm now overdressed," James murmured and promptly shrugged off his jacket. Fire burned in the depths of his gaze as he shucked his waistcoat next.

Abigail stared. She'd never seen him with so few clothes on before, and the thought of soon watching him strip off the rest sent a thrill through her veins that heated her blood. "Perhaps if I take off my stays you'll remove your shirt?"

His nostrils flared. "Turn around so I can untie you."

She didn't hesitate, and then she felt his fingers tickling the back of her neck as he unpinned her hair. A delicious series of shivers swept the length of her spine. It almost felt like his fingers trembled against her skin as he swept the fallen locks aside and went to work on the laces. Her stays fell to the floor; a bit of cool air came between her and James, followed by a low rustling sound. And then she felt him, his warm chest against her back, his bare arms caging her, and his lips kissing the curve of her shoulder.

Instinctively, she leaned back against him and savored the slow slide of his hands as he started exploring her body. The way he smelled, of spice, brandy, and a hint of sandalwood, was so heady she sighed with the pleasure of breathing the masculine scent. He answered with a low growl and began pulling her chemise up over her thighs.

"You're everything I've ever dreamed of," he told her, then scraped her skin with his teeth in a way that caused hot desire to burn low in her belly. "Everything I need and all that I want." Hands splayed so they touched as much of her body as possibly, he slid her chemise even higher, until she raised her arms and he was able to sweep it up over her head.

With aching slowness, he trailed one fingertip down the length of her back and over the curve of her bottom. She sucked in a breath when his hand fell away and was stunned to realize how desperate she was for a far more intimate touch.

"James," was the only word she could manage, and even that sounded more like a breathy caress than actual speech.

His hands moved to her hips and as he turned her toward him, she barely managed to catch the hungry look in his eyes before his mouth was on hers. Somehow, he managed to deepen the kiss while removing his trousers and still keeping one hand firmly planted on her waist. He tasted incredible, of decadent pleasure and sinful adventure.

"I'll make it good for you, Abby," he promised as he swept her up into his arms and carried her to the bed.

"You already are," she whispered, feeling suddenly shy when he laid her down and took a moment to let his gaze sweep the length of her body.

She looked at him too, though only out of the corner of her eye since her curiosity embarrassed her slightly. And what she saw almost stole her breath, for his naked physique was the most magnificent thing she'd ever seen.

His chest, sculpted with peaks and valleys in all the right places, rose and fell in accordance with his breaths. "You can't imagine how much I want you." The chords at his throat seemed to strain, and when he reached down to cover her breast with his hand, she saw that the muscles in his arms were tense.

"I want you too," she told him in earnest, her words filling the space between them with hungry anticipation.

An almost primal expression captured his features. "My god, Abby." The utterance seemed to be torn from his throat as he climbed onto the bed beside her. "I don't want to hurt you or frighten you, but I need you so damn much and I'll try...I promise I'll try to go slow but—"

"Shh..." Her hand found his cheek where unshaved bristles provided a curiously satisfying bit of abrasion. "Forget your concerns and just love me, James. That's all I ask."

So he did. Pressing soft kisses to every part of her body and caressing her with his hands, he stoked the fire of her need until she begged for more. And when she grew tense in response to their joining, he stopped to let her adjust, and then forced her attention away from the pain with a kiss that outdid the rest.

"I love you," he said once again when they found a shared rhythm. Braced above her, he held her gaze with fierce intensity while taking her to some unexplored place she'd never before known existed.

A wonderful pressure comprised of tingling heat formed at her core, building and expanding until she gasped with the need for something she couldn't explain. And then it exploded, flinging her body straight up to the stars and blinding her with a flash of bright light. "Oh god, James," she shouted and opened her eyes to see that his head was flung back as he uttered a primitive growl.

Warm sparks of pleasure kept rippling through her for some time after, and then a relaxing languor filled her limbs.

James exhaled a series of breaths. "Christ, Abby." He stared at her for a moment in wonder, then settled his mouth over hers for a tender kiss. Lowering himself to the spot beside her on the mattress, he rolled over onto his side and pulled her into his arms. "That," he murmured against her ear, "was incredible."

"I have to agree," she said with a smile both on her lips and in her heart. "So incredible, in fact, that I think I might like to do it again as soon as possible."

Grinning, he reached for her hand and wove his fingers together with hers. And as he did so, Abby knew the life they were going to have would be nothing short of spectacular. James had helped her vanquish her fears, and the love they now shared, based on friendship, trust, and mutual respect, was powerful enough to conquer the world.

Thank you so much for taking the time to read the second book in my Townsbridge novella series. If you enjoyed *Lady Abigail's Perfect Match*, you'll definitely enjoy the prequel. Grab your copy of *When Love Leads to Scandal* today so you don't miss out on Caleb's and Bethany's story! Or check out the sequel. *Falling for Mr. Townsbridge* has William falling for his mother's new cook, so if you like Cinderella style romances this is the book for you!

And don't miss *No Ordinary Duke*! This is the first book in The Crawfords series and features a newly minted duke who just wants to live a normal life and a woman who despises the aristocracy. When sparks fly between them and she discovers his true identity, compromises must be made if they're to stand a chance of a happily ever after together.

Or if you're looking for a longer read, why not try *The Forgotten Duke*? In this *Diamonds In The Rough* story, Lady Regina Berkly flees her wedding and turns to Carlton Guthrie, the Scoundrel of St. Giles, for help. There is no doubt in her mind that falling for him would be a mistake, and yet there's something about this man – something so tempting she cannot resist. What she doesn't know, is that his kindness toward her is not only linked to desire, but to an all-consuming need for revenge.

You can find out more about my new releases, backlist deals and giveaways by signing up for my newsletter on www.sophiebarnes.com And don't forget to follow me on Facebook for even more updates and fun book related posts and on BookBub for new release alerts and deals.

Once again, I thank you for your interest in my books. Please take a moment to leave a review since this can help other readers discover my books. And please continue reading for an excerpt from *Falling for Mr. Townsbridge*.

Falling for Mr. Townsbridge

The Townsbridges

Chapter One

EVEN THOUGH THE LONDON air was soaked with fine droplets of rain, it was still good to be home. Stepping down from the carriage, William Townsbridge paused to study the red brick townhouse with its white window casings. Beads of water gathered like dew drops upon his coat. A wry smile touched his lips. The delight he felt right now would most likely fade the moment he stepped through the front door and met his mother, Margaret, Viscountess Roxley.

As much as he loved her, he had no desire to be her marital project, which was part of the reason he kept on leaving. The last time he'd been home she'd kept on reminding him that his brothers had both married when they'd been six and twenty.

William had been one year younger than that at the time, but his mother had clearly believed it was time to prepare – for him to begin considering potential matches so he'd be ready to strike as soon as his next birthday came. It had passed with little fuss since he'd deliberately been away, working as the aide to the British ambassador in Lisbon. Before that, his father, Lord Roxley, had helped him travel to America with the excuse of exploring new investment opportunities.

Prepared for what was to come, William helped the coachman unload his luggage, paid the man, and went to knock on the door. He'd already made plans to go away again in a month to visit a friend's holiday home in Florence. Until then, he'd simply grit his teeth and nod whenever some young lady's name was mentioned, while savoring the bone deep knowledge that his mother meant well. She loved him and simply wanted him to find the kind of happiness she enjoyed with his father and which his brothers had also been lucky to find with their wives.

Grabbing the knocker, William gave the door three loud raps and grinned when his youngest sister, Athena, came to greet him instead of Simmons, the butler.

Athena's eyes widened. A laugh escaped her. And then her arms were around his neck in a fierce hug. "You're back. Oh thank heavens. Sarah and I have missed you dreadfully, William. She more than I, I'm sure. My goodness, she'll be thrilled to have you home. You've no idea. No idea at all."

An odd sense of foreboding crept under William's skin. "What do you mean?"

Athena grabbed his arm and pulled him more fully into the foyer so they could shut the door. An exaggerated sigh of despair escaped her. And then she rolled her eyes. Although she was old enough now at the age of twenty for him to consider her a fully grown woman, her boisterous energy still made him think of her as a child.

"Mama is being impossible."

The whispered piece of information was barely spoken before the door to the parlor opened and the lady herself appeared. She was followed by her husband and William's other sister, Sarah. He met Sarah's gaze and barely managed to give her a quick smile before he was swept into his mother's arms.

"We've missed you," she said.

"I've missed you too," William told her loyally.

They broke apart just as Simmons made his appearance. "My apologies for not arriving sooner. It's good to see you again, Mr. Townsbridge. Please, allow me to take your bags."

"Thank you." William handed over his things, greeted his father with a solid handshake and Sarah with another embrace.

"Come," his mother said. "We'll call for some tea and a snack to tide you over until dinner."

"You're in for a treat," Athena said, traipsing behind as the family left the foyer. "Mama has hired a new cook. Mrs. Lamont is her name and everything she makes is utterly divine."

William glanced at his father. Neither had ever cared much for food one way or the other. Eating was just a necessity – an inconvenience that got in the way of whatever else they'd rather be doing. And dinners always lasted ten times longer than William believed necessary.

"She's not wrong," Roxley said, much to William's surprise. "I actually look forward to meals now, if you can believe it."

Incredulous, William stared at his father for a moment. "Well, I suppose I'll have to decide for myself."

"But before you do, I'd like to hear your opinion on Sarah's potential suitors," William's mother said. Everyone groaned, including Roxley, but she was determined. "There's Viscount Belmont, Mr. Hastings, the Earl of Penwood, the Earl of Endry, Mr. Cummings, Mr. Dunnings, Mr—"

William stared at his mother while she continued to tick names off on her fingers. Five minutes later, he understood exactly why Sarah and Athena were so glad to have him home. They clearly hoped his presence would help distract their mother from her desire to get them settled by focusing more energy on him.

Ha! Not if he could help it. Although he really did pity his sisters. He knew how relentless Mama could be, and unlike him, they weren't able to run away. But there was something wonderfully entertaining about watching someone else deal with her matchmaking efforts for a change.

William waited until she was done before saying, "I'm sorry, I forgot the first few names. Could you please repeat them?"

The viscountess knit her brow but proceeded to do so while everyone else glared at him. Athena looked like she'd like to grab the nearest throw pillow and hit him over the head with it. He suppressed a chuckle.

"Well?" his mother finally asked once she'd gone over all the names again. Tea had been served in the meantime, and a plate filled with interesting looking pastries had been placed on the table before him.

William picked one up, took a bite...

Oh dear God in heaven.

Rich cream laced with a hint of lemon burst from within the fluffy dough and filled his mouth with blissful pleasure. He groaned – *groaned* – and closed his eyes in acknowledgement of the divine moment.

"Good. Isn't it?" Athena asked.

When William opened his eyes, she was watching him slyly while sinking her teeth into her own piece of perfection.

He nodded. "I don't think I've ever had anything this good before."

"Papa insists Mrs. Lamont must be a witch," Sarah said while she selected a treat and passed the plate to her father.

"It does seem like the only logical explanation," Roxley said, his eyes almost rolling all the way back in his head when he took a bite of the pastry he'd picked.

William ate some more and immediately lamented the loss of the treat once he'd finished off the last bite. "Why aren't there more?" he grumbled.

His mother chuckled. "Because it would spoil our appetites for dinner. Have some tea, dear, and tell me your thoughts."

"It's incredible," William said. "If everything Mrs. Lamont makes is as good this, you must be the envy of all of London."

"Try England," Roxley said.

"And I wasn't referring to the pastries," the viscountess said with a hint of impatience. "What I wish to know is which man you think might be best for Sarah. And possibly for Athena as well."

"Please leave me out of this," Athena grumbled.

"I don't see why my opinion should matter," William said. He picked up his cup and sipped his tea while offering Sarah a look of apology.

"He – the man she marries – will become your brother-in-law," Mama explained. "You'll have to spend time with him at family gatherings and—"

"To be clear," William said, determined more than ever to put an end to this arduous conversation, "my only concern is for Sarah's happiness. She could choose to marry a troll, and I'd still be cordial to the fellow."

Athena snorted with laughter, earning a stern look of disapproval from both parents.

Sarah's lips twitched. "Thank you, Will."

"A troll indeed," their mother sputtered. She looked monumentally put out.

"Right then," William said, deciding to take advantage of her brief silence. "I think I shall go wash up and prepare for dinner."

"I'll do the same," Athena said.

"Me too," Sarah added.

"See you in roughly one hour," William told his parents.

He followed his sisters into the hallway and was halfway up the stairs before his father's startled expression registered. The poor man was now Mama's only audience, and William fleetingly wondered if he ought to feel some remorse over this. So he paused, glanced back down at the parlor door, and finally chose to continue his climb. Roxley loved his wife to distraction. He'd chosen to spend the rest of his life with her. And there was no way in hell William was going back in the parlor right now.

Instead, he took his time reacquainting himself with his bedroom. The books he'd enjoyed as a child still sat on top of his dresser in a neat collection of sentimentality. The pocket watch he'd received from Grandfather John on his fifteenth birthday gleamed in greeting when he opened the top drawer. A smile curved his lips as he pulled the watch into the palm of his hand. Grandfather John's sweet tooth had been undeniable. He would have loved those delicious pastries. The flavor still lingered on William's tongue, prompting him to ponder the woman who'd made them.

With a smile and a shake of his head, he returned the watch to the drawer for safe keeping and pulled out a neatly folded shirt. She was probably much like all the other cooks he'd ever seen: middle-aged and plump with a cheerful disposition. And most likely married to a very happy man, William decided with a grin.

This opinion did not change when he joined his family for dinner and savored his first bite of seafood mousse topped with dill and lemon. Or when a plate containing perfectly grilled slices of beef tenderloin was placed before him. The succulent meat melted in his mouth along with the baby potatoes and baked vegetables. And when the dessert arrived...

Ah, but it was yet another culinary masterpiece – a chocolate cake of some sort filled with nuts, so moist and sweet he wished he had several more stomachs to fill.

"Judging from that look on your face, I gather you will be staying a while," his mother teased.

"If you're wise," he told her dryly, deciding not to ruin the mood by addressing his plans for departure, "you will lock Mrs. Lamont away before someone steals her."

"I think you ought to meet her," Athena said.

Roxley coughed while their mother and Sarah both stared at her in dismay. William felt as though he might be missing something – a joke perhaps?

"I'm sure William has more important things do," Roxley managed to say while still clearing his throat. "Like calling on his brothers."

"It was just a suggestion," Athena muttered.

"And we thank you for it," Mama said in that firm tone meant to put an end to a subject, "but Mrs. Lamont takes her cooking extremely seriously. I'm sure she would hate to be disturbed."

The pointed look that followed gave William pause. He frowned. Something was up. His mother's tight smile, Roxley shifting the conversation to what William's exact duties had been at the embassy in Lisbon, the attention Sarah was giving her plate, and the mutinous look in Athena's eyes all suggested they were hiding something.

Naturally, he meant to learn what it was. Which was why he allowed his father to invite him to his study for an after dinner drink, indulged him in whatever topics he wished to discuss, enjoyed a cup of tea afterward with his mother and sisters in the parlor, then excused himself and headed for bed.

Once in his room he waited until he was sure the rest of his family had retired as well, and then headed straight for the kitchen.

THERE WAS SOMETHING immensely satisfying about having the kitchen all to herself once the rest of the servants had gone up to bed. Eloise loved it. The Townsbridge House kitchen was large, beautifully fitted with everything a cook or a chef might desire. This was her favorite time of day – after the hustle and bustle – when she could prepare the next day's meals, partly in her head and partly by jotting down some of the items she'd have to purchase the following morning.

A smile stole across her lips as she sat at the work table with her notebook and pencil. She never trusted another person to shop on her behalf. This was something *Grand-père* Victor had taught her. Every part of every meal was her *responsabilité*, and as such, it was up to her to select the finest ingredients possible.

Taking a sip of the sweet mint tea she'd prepared, she made a few notes. If she was going to prepare her grandfather's specialty, she'd have to buy some fresh mushrooms. Perhaps some asparagus too. And a vanilla pod, if she was able to find one, for the dessert.

Eloise had almost finished jotting down the items when a soft scrape drew her attention. She looked up and paused. A man stood in the far corner of the room, just inside the doorway. Tall, with chiseled features, dark hair, a firm mouth, and a curious gaze, he was both handsome and intimidating all at once.

"Who are you?" Eloise blurted, even though she suspected she already knew the answer. Simmons had mentioned the arrival of the youngest Townsbridge son, so she supposed this would have to be him.

"Who are you?" he asked, echoing her words without giving an answer.

Eloise set down her pencil and stood. It was the polite thing to do, not to mention that he might not seem quite so tall if she weren't sitting. Of course she was wrong about that. She realized this as he crossed the floor, growing in size as he approached.

It was tempting to take a step back, to retreat and add distance. But that would only reveal how unnerving she found him. Her heart fluttered against her breast. It would show weakness while giving him the upper hand.

So she straightened her spine instead and raised her chin. "Mrs. Lamont," she told him. "I am *la cuisinière*. The cook."

He stared at her so long she started to wonder if she had flour in her hair or a smudge of sauce on her cheek. And then he smiled, slow and with wolfish delight.

A shiver raced through Eloise. She balled her hands into two tight fists. To respond in any way, if even with the briefest pleasure of his regard, was unconscionable and dangerous.

"You made those incredible cream pastries I tasted this afternoon?" he asked. She nodded. Once. "And dinner as well?"

"*Oui*."

Amazement brightened his eyes to a rich shade of walnut. "I must say, I'm thoroughly impressed. More so now that I've met you."

Eloise frowned. It bothered her that she always had to prove herself on account of her age. Lady Roxley had been hesitant, too, about hiring her, and Eloise had practically been forced to beg for a chance to show off her skills.

"Not what you expected?"

"Not at all."

She flattened her mouth. "Well, you're not what I expected either."

The words were out before she could stop them, hanging in the air like a challenge. Why had she said that? What on earth was she thinking?

"Explain." He crossed his arms and arched a brow.

Eloise fought to maintain her composure. Somehow she'd lost all common sense and walked straight into battle. And of course she was far too stubborn to back down now. So she ignored the voice of reason encouraging her to retreat.

Instead, she said, "Having met your brothers, I imagined you would be just as polite and charming as they are. Instead you barge in here—" a slight exaggeration, she had to admit "–intruding on my domain, as if it is your right to do so."

Mr. Townsbridge blinked. "So you know who I am."

She crossed her arms and gave him a very deliberate head-to-toe perusal. "It isn't hard to figure out."

"Then you must know I live here." He was speaking to her as if she were an infant now.

Eloise supposed she deserved it, but his manner still made her jaw clench. "Fleetingly, perhaps. As a guest."

"Townsbridge House is my home when I am in England. It is the only permanent address I have." He leaned forward. "I've certainly spent more time here than you. In response to that other comment you made, you should know that I intend to roam about as I see fit, Mrs. Lamont. No room in this house is off limits to me. Not even..."

Eloise gasped. Her eyes widened while heat rose to her cheeks.

"The kitchen," he finished with a devilish smirk.

Anger flared within her, hot and prickly. The cad had been about to say, *not even yours*. She knew it as surely as she knew how to ice a cake or bake a soufflé. The arrogant mockery in his eyes was proof enough.

Initially, she'd wanted him gone because he'd been too attractive. The last thing she wanted was for some foolish fancy to get in the way of her work. Except she'd been wrong to worry. Mr. Townsbridge was a beastly man – certainly not the sort who'd ever inspire more tender feelings within her.

A pity, since it meant his looks had been wasted.

Eloise grabbed her shopping list. "I think it's time for us to bid each other good night."

"If that is your wish," he said, turning away as if he'd lost interest in her. "I'll just fix myself a quick snack before I head back upstairs."

"The devil you will," Eloise exploded.

She froze as the words she'd spoken settled around her. Mr. Townsbridge swung back and pinned her in place with the most intense gaze she had even been subjected to.

"My," he murmured, "you are a feisty thing."

Eloise gulped. *Remember your place.* "For—" she cleared her throat and tried again "—forgive me. That was intolerably rude."

A slow smile slid into place on his face. "I probably ought to apologize too. For the teasing. It clearly made you uncomfortable."

She managed a stiff nod. Spending more time in his company was an incredibly bad idea, but the thought of him or anyone else rummaging through her cupboards was somehow worse.

Which was the only reason why she found herself saying, "Allow me to fix you a plate."

"Thank you. But I can manage."

"Not if you wish to leave this kitchen in one piece you can't."

He laughed, quite suddenly and with a shocking degree of mirth. Eloise pressed her lips together until her own laughter forced them apart.

"I can vividly imagine you chasing me with a rolling pin or a frying pan," he choked.

"The carving knife has just been sharpened," she said.

"Good God. You're not just a spitfire or a good cook, you're also a bloodthirsty hellion." He stepped back in mock terror. "No wonder my parents and sisters were trying to hide you. They must have feared for my life."

"They certainly have better sense than to try and meddle with my supplies." Although the truth was, Eloise had come to adore the family. They were kind and generous. She'd even begun considering Lady Athena her friend after they'd started spending their Sunday mornings together. And she appreciated the brief chats she occasionally had with Lady Roxley whenever the viscountess wished to check up on meal plans.

Giving Mr. Townsbridge a wide berth, Eloise pocketed her shopping list and went to the cupboard. "Will a lemon cream puff do?"

"Make it two and we have a deal," Mr. Townsbridge told her.

Eloise deliberately kept her back toward him as she smiled. "It's *your* waistline, *monsieur*, not mine."

"The things you say," he muttered with a hint of wonder. "You're quite unlike any other servant I've ever met."

Collecting a plate, Eloise retrieved the tin containing the leftover pastries and pulled off the lid. Risking a glance in his direction she told him wryly, "I'm French. Meekness is not in my blood."

A spark of awareness flared to life in his eyes, prompting her to drop her gaze quickly. She finished preparing his plate and handed it to him. His thumb brushed hers and her heart leapt. This was wrong, this response she was having toward him. Nothing about it made sense when only moments ago she'd been ready to hit him.

Avoiding further eye contact, she busied herself with putting the tin away. "I have an early morning so I must be off now."

"Won't you keep me company while I eat?"

Eloise swallowed. "*Non*." She closed the cupboard and forced her feet to move toward the door. Reaching it, she paused to say, "It was interesting to meet you, Mr. Townsbridge. I hope you enjoy your snack."

She turned away.

"I trust your husband is also in my parents' employ?"

"No. I'm not..." Too late, she realized what she'd revealed. Cooks were always referred to as Mrs., no matter their marital status, and keeping Mr. Townsbridge in the dark about hers would have served as a useful line of defense. If she'd been wise enough to leave him wondering, that was, or even better if she'd lied.

"Duly noted."

The comment chased her out of the kitchen and into the servants' stairwell, all the way up to her room on the top floor of the house. She didn't pause for breath until she was safely inside with the door shut. Good heavens. The way he'd said that, with seductive promise, was enough to set her ablaze.

She patted her cheeks and expelled a deep breath.

No.

She absolutely could not allow herself to be alone with that man ever again. Not only because of the threat he posed to her job but because of what she feared he might want. And judging by how quickly he'd replaced her indignation with amusement, she worried he had the skill to acquire whatever he might desire.

Which meant she would have to avoid him at all cost.

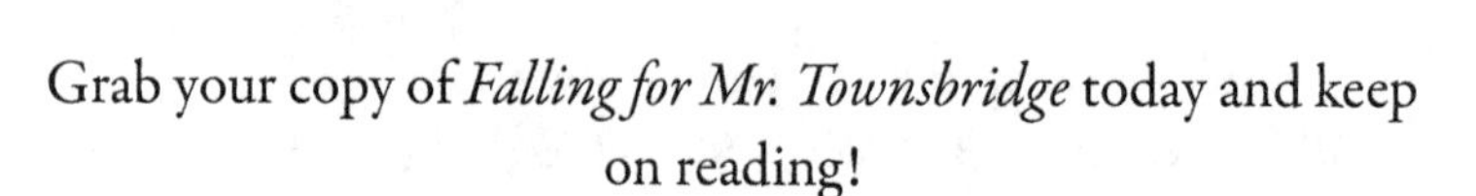

Grab your copy of *Falling for Mr. Townsbridge* today and keep on reading!

Acknowledgments

I WOULD LIKE TO THANK the Killion Group for their incredible help with the editing, formatting and cover design of this book. And to my friends and family, thank you for your constant support. I would be lost without you!

About The Author

Born in Denmark, Sophie has spent her youth traveling with her parents to wonderful places around the world. She's lived in five different countries, on three different continents, has studied design in Paris and New York, and has a bachelor's degree from Parson's School of design. But most impressive of all - she's been married to the same man three times, in three different countries and in three different dresses.

While living in Africa, Sophie turned to her lifelong passion - writing.

When she's not busy, dreaming up her next romance novel, Sophie enjoys spending time with her family, swimming, cooking, gardening, watching romantic comedies and, of course, reading. She currently lives on the East Coast.

You can contact her through her website at www.sophiebarnes.com

And please consider leaving a review for this book.

Reviews help readers find books, so every review is greatly appreciated!

Don't miss out!

Visit the website below and you can sign up to receive emails whenever Sophie Barnes publishes a new book. There's no charge and no obligation.

https://books2read.com/r/B-A-FJPE-AHSBB

BOOKS 2 READ

Connecting independent readers to independent writers.

CPSIA information can be obtained
at www.ICGtesting.com
Printed in the USA
LVHW032346240121
677394LV00046B/718